PUFFIN BOOKS

Editor: Kaye Webb

KEEPING UP WITH TEDDY ROBINSON

None of Deborah's other toys was quite as comforting and friendly as dear cuddly Teddy Robinson, with his nice round tummy, his smart tartan trousers and the fur that was all worn away round his nose with so much kissing.

Teddy Robinson was really quite a stay-at-home character, his short legs not being much use for walking, but adventures seemed to come his way all the same. Once, for instance, Deborah left him outside a shop and he was carried away in a strange baby's pram, and another time he was sold by mistake in a jumble sale! But wherever he was, in a litter-bin maybe, a bird cage, or an unknown lady's shopping bag, Teddy Robinson's happy, hopeful nature carried him safely through.

The nine stories in this book are just right for reading aloud, and have all the warmth and charm of the other Young Puffin Teddy Robinson books, *About Teddy Robinson*, *Dear Teddy Robinson*, and *Teddy Robinson Himself*, which have put countless little children firmly under the spell of one of the very nicest teddy bears.

For readers of four and over.

Keeping Up with Teddy Robinson

Written and illustrated by

Joan G. Robinson

PUFFIN BOOKS

Puffin Books, Penguin Books Ltd, Harmondsworth, Middlesex, England
Penguin Books Inc., 7110 Ambassador Road, Baltimore, Maryland 21207, U.S.A.
Penguin Books Australia Ltd, Ringwood, Victoria, Australia
Penguin Books Canada Ltd, 41 Steelcase Road West, Markham, Ontario, Canada
Penguin Books (N.Z.) Ltd, 182–190 Wairau Road, Auckland 10, New Zealand

—

First published by Harrap 1964
Published in Puffin Books 1975 with additional stories: 'Teddy Robinson and
the Teddy-bear Brooch', 'Teddy Robinson and the Fairies', and 'Teddy Robinson's
Dreadful Accident' (from *More About Teddy Robinson*, 1954) and 'Teddy Robinson
Has a Holiday' (from *Teddy Robinson's Book*, 1955)

—

Copyright © Joan G. Robinson, 1954, 1955, 1964

—

Made and printed in Great Britain by
Richard Clay (The Chaucer Press) Ltd, Bungay, Suffolk
Set in Monotype Imprint

Contents

For
Gregory Hugo

I

Teddy Robinson Tries to Keep Up

TEDDY ROBINSON was a nice, big, comfortable, friendly teddy bear. He had light-brown fur and kind brown eyes, and he belonged to a little girl called Deborah.

One day Teddy Robinson was sitting in Deborah's window, looking across the road, when he suddenly saw something very odd. In the window of the house opposite he saw himself looking out.

'Fancy that,' said Teddy Robinson, 'I never knew I was reflected in that window.' And he sat up a little straighter and began to admire himself quietly.

'My fur looks better than I thought,' he said to himself. 'The part that's been kissed away all round my nose hardly shows from here. And my trousers aren't too shabby at all. I'm really quite a handsome bear from a distance.' And he was pleased to think the people over the road had such a fine view of him.

But a little later, when he looked across again, he had another surprise. He could see quite clearly in the reflection of the window opposite that he had a hat on. A large, round, red beret with a bobble on top.

'That's funny,' he said to himself. 'I don't re-member Deborah putting my hat on. Anyway my hat doesn't look like that. Can she have bought me a new

— a large, round, red beret with a bobble on top.

one, and put it on my head when I wasn't looking?'
Just then Deborah came running in.

'Hallo,' said Teddy Robinson. 'Why have I got
this hat on?'

'What hat?' said Deborah, surprised.

'Haven't I got a hat on?' said Teddy Robinson.
'A large, round, red beret with a bobble on top?'

'No, of course you haven't,' said Deborah, and
she came over and looked at him closely.

'Look over there, then,' said Teddy Robinson.
'Isn't that me? And haven't I got a hat on?'

Deborah looked. 'Oh, that's funny!' she said.

'They've got a teddy bear just like you! He's even got the same sort of trousers. I wonder why they put him up in the window.'

'Was it to show off that hat?' said Teddy Robinson.

'Yes, perhaps it was,' said Deborah. 'That big girl, Pauline Jones, lives there. The one who goes to school and wears a uniform. That's her hat.'

'It's a very nice hat,' said Teddy Robinson.

'Yes,' said Deborah, 'but I wish the girl was nice too. She's not a bit friendly. Once when I took you out in the dolls' pram she stared hard, but she never even smiled at us. When *I* go to a big school with a uniform I shan't be like that. I'll say hallo to everybody, no matter how young they are.'

Teddy Robinson stared across at the other bear.

'I'd better have my hat on,' he said.

'Yes, they may as well see you've got one too,' said Deborah, and she fetched his knitted bonnet.

'Where are my other hats?' said Teddy Robinson.

'You haven't any, you know that,' said Deborah. 'But this is lovely, it's a real baby's bonnet.'

'Yes, I was afraid it was,' said Teddy Robinson. 'Can't you lend me one of yours?'

So Deborah fetched one of her own hats. It had poppies and corn round it, and ribbon streamers.

'That's much better!' said Teddy Robinson. 'Now, haven't I got a paper sunshade as well?'

'Oh, yes!' said Deborah. 'What fun!'

And a few minutes later Teddy Robinson was sitting proudly in the window, with Deborah's best hat on and his paper sunshade over his head.

Deborah was just having tea when she heard Teddy Robinson shouting, 'Can I have something to eat? That bear over the road has got an orange!'

She ran in with her slice of bread and butter. It had a big bite taken out of it. She propped it up on Teddy Robinson's paw against the window, then went back to finish her tea. But a moment later Teddy Robinson called out again.

'Hey! That Jones bear has got a bun now!'

Deborah ran in again, this time with a slice of cake in her hand. She propped it up on his other paw.

'Now are you happy?' she said.

—sitting proudly in the window
with Deborah's best hat on—

'Oh, yes, thank you,' said Teddy Robinson.

But when Deborah came back again after tea, Teddy Robinson was looking gloomy.

'*Now* what's the matter?' she said.

'I don't like tea with nothing to drink,' said Teddy Robinson.

Deborah looked across at the other window and saw that the Jones bear now had a bottle of milk in front of him, with a straw sticking out of it.

'Oh dear,' she said, 'poor Teddy Robinson! I'd better get the dolls' tea-set out.'

And soon Teddy Robinson was sitting with his tea nicely laid out in front of him on a tray.

'This *is* fun!' said Deborah. 'I do wonder who is doing it. Surely it can't be that girl, Pauline, who never even says hallo?'

Teddy Robinson didn't know who it was either. He tried to keep watch to see if he could see anyone moving about, but somehow he always just missed it.

Next time he looked he saw that the milk bottle had gone, and the bear was now reading a book.

'Bring me a book, Deborah!' he shouted. 'A big book. The biggest you can find!'

Deborah came running in with the telephone book and propped it up in front of him on the toy blackboard. It was very dull, with nothing but long lists of names in it, but luckily Teddy Robinson couldn't read, so he didn't know how bored he was. And it was fun trying to keep up with the other bear.

'He doesn't even know I can't read,' he said, and chuckled to himself.

But by bedtime he was getting quite stiff.

'Thank goodness I can get down now,' he said. Then he looked across at the other house. A big dolls' cot had just been put on the window sill!

'Oh, my goodness!' he said, 'what ever next?' Then he shouted loudly, 'A bed! Bring me a bed!'

Deborah came running. 'What is it now?'

'I must have a bed!' said Teddy Robinson. 'A bed all to myself. At once!'

'That's not a very nice way to ask,' said Deborah.

'Please, dear Deborah, may I have a bed all of my own?' said Teddy Robinson. 'I can't possibly let that Jones bear know I haven't got one.'

Deborah rummaged in the toy cupboard and pulled out an old dolls' bed. 'It's too small,' she said.

'And the bottom's fallen out,' said Teddy Robinson.

'But it's all we've got,' said Deborah.

'Then it'll have to do,' said Teddy Robinson. 'Put my nightie on quickly and squeeze me in.'

So Deborah did. Then she covered him with a doll's blanket, put the telephone book underneath, to stop him falling through, and put him up on the sill.

'Are you comfy?' she said.

'No, thank you,' said Teddy Robinson. 'But at least I'm glad I've got a proper nightie, and don't have to go to bed in my trousers.'

'I wonder if they can see it,' said Deborah.

'Shall we hang my trousers up?' said Teddy Robinson. 'Then they'll know I haven't got them on.'

So Deborah found a dress hanger, and hung Teddy Robinson's trousers up in the window for every one to see. And Teddy Robinson lay underneath and thought how funny they looked without him inside them.

Then Deborah kissed him and got into her own bed. Usually Teddy Robinson slept there too. Sometimes he pushed his way down in the night until he

— and thought how funny they looked without him inside them —

was right at the bottom of the bed and as warm as toast. But tonight he was very cold. The blanket was far too small, and he couldn't move an inch.

He had a dreadful night.

When at last Deborah came for him in the morning, he was too stiff and sleepy to sit up straight.

But Deborah was very bright. She said, 'Oh, do look! The Jones bear is having breakfast now!'

Sure enough, there he sat in the window with a big packet of cornflakes in front of him.

'I'd better have eggs and bacon then, hadn't I?' said Teddy Robinson, waking up.

'No,' said Deborah, 'let's pretend you had breakfast in bed. Then while I'm having mine, you can be thinking of something to do afterwards.'

But when she came back after breakfast Teddy Robinson was sitting all humped up, and she could tell by the look of his back that he was feeling sad.

'Haven't you thought of anything?' she said.

'No,' said Teddy Robinson, 'and I'm not going to. I'm tired of trying to keep up with the Joneses. They go too quickly for me. Look over there now.'

Deborah looked across and saw that the Jones bear was now wearing a shiny blue party dress with big puffed sleeves, and a blue satin ribbon, tied in a bow between the ears.

'Oh dear,' she said, 'we haven't anything as grand as that. Shall I put on your best purple dress?'

'No,' said Teddy Robinson sadly. 'Did you see what he's got beside him?'

Deborah looked again. 'Oh! A dear little dolls' sewing machine! *Aren't* they lucky?'

'Turn me round,' said Teddy Robinson. 'I shan't look any more. I think he's showing off. I don't like bears who put on airs.' And he began singing, with his back to the window.

> 'Teddy bears
> who put on airs
> are not the bears for me.
> Bears are best
> not over-dressed –
> in pants, perhaps,
> or just a vest,
> but *not* the clothes you wear for best –
> they're better fat and free.
>
> A friendly, free-and-easy bear,
> a cosy, jolly, teasy bear
> is always welcome
> everywhere.
> Fair and furry,
> fat and free,
> *that's* the kind of bear to be.
> Like me.'

After that he stuck his tummy out again and began to feel better.

'Lift me down,' he said to Deborah. 'If that Jones bear only wants to see what things I've got, then he doesn't need to see *me* at all. We can leave all my things in the window for him to look at, and then go off on our own to a desert island and be very happy with nothing at all. Why didn't I think of it before?'

So quickly they arranged all his things in the window. They hung up his nightie, his best purple dress and his trousers on three little dress hangers. They hung his paper sunshade and his knitted bonnet from the window latch. Then they took a sheet of cardboard and Deborah wrote on it in big black letters,

GONE AWAY FROM IT ALL

and they propped it up in front of the window on the toy blackboard. Then they went away.

Hours later Teddy Robinson was lying on his back in the middle of a small round flower bed in the garden. He had no clothes on at all, and a gentle breeze ruffled the fur on his tummy. He sighed happily, staring up at the lupins as they waved gently over his head, and sang to himself softly,

> 'Lucky bear,
> lucky bear,
> all alone
> and free as air.
> No more things
> to bother me,
> lucky me,
> lucky me.
> Free-and-easy,
> fat and free,
> what a lucky bear I be . . .'

'All the same,' he said to himself, 'I wish I had

somebody else to be all alone and lucky with. That Jones bear would have done, if only he hadn't been so proud, showing off with all his things.'

Just then he heard Mummy calling to Deborah.

'Listen,' she said, 'I've just met Mrs Jones who lives opposite, and what do you think she said? She asked me why Teddy Robinson had gone away! I told her he hadn't, and she said, "Well, that's funny, my Pauline said he had, and she's so sad about it."'

'But why is she sad?' said Deborah.

'Mrs Jones says Pauline is very shy and finds it hard to make friends,' said Mummy. 'She's often seen you two together and wanted to talk to you, but she was too shy. Then when her birthday came she asked for a teddy bear like yours. Mrs Jones thought she was too old for it now she goes to a big school. But Pauline wanted it so much that she bought her one. And she says she has been so happy playing with you and Teddy Robinson, and she'd hoped you were going to be friends. Isn't it funny?'

Then Deborah told Mummy all about it. And a little later she went over to Pauline's house.

Teddy Robinson said, 'Fancy that!' to himself three times over, and fell asleep in the sunshine.

When he woke up again, Deborah and Pauline were peering down at him through the lupins.

'There he is,' said Deborah. 'Don't tell, but this is his desert island. Let's put Teddy Jones down with him, then they can get to know each other.'

So Teddy Jones had his party dress taken off and was put down beside Teddy Robinson. Then Pauline and Deborah ran off to play.

The two teddy bears lay on their backs and looked at each other sideways.

'Nice to lie down, isn't it?' said Teddy Robinson.

'*Very* nice,' said Teddy Jones, with a cosy grunt.

'I must say I got a bit stiff sitting up in that window,' said Teddy Robinson.

'So did I,' said Teddy Jones. 'This is a nice little place you've got here.'

'Yes, it's my desert island,' said Teddy Robinson. 'Have you got one?'

'Oh, don't start all that again!' said Teddy Jones. 'I'm worn out trying to keep up with you!'

'What!' said Teddy Robinson. 'You can't be as worn out as I am. That's why I'm lying here. I nearly broke my back in that awful little bed.'

'You may as well know I wasn't as comfortable as I looked,' said Teddy Jones. 'That cot was too small. I had a shocking night.'

'*Did* you?' said Teddy Robinson. 'Oh, I *am* glad! But I bet mine was worse; my bed had no bottom to it.'

'Now I'll tell *you* something,' said Teddy Jones. 'That hat wasn't mine. I borrowed it.'

'Mine wasn't mine either,' said Teddy Robinson. 'I only borrowed it to keep up with you.'

'But why?' said Teddy Jones. 'Fancy a proud sort of chap like you trying to keep up with me!'

'*I'm* not a proud sort of chap,' said Teddy Robinson. 'I thought you were. I'm only me.'

"we don't have to bother any more."

'And I'm only me,' said Teddy Jones.

'Well now, isn't that nice?' said Teddy Robinson. 'If you're only you and I'm only me, we don't have to bother any more.'

'And we might even come to tea with each other instead?' said Teddy Jones.

'Yes, of course!' said Teddy Robinson. 'What a silly old sausage of a bear I am! I've been so busy trying to show off to you with all the things I haven't got, that I quite forgot to make friends with you. You come to tea with me today, and I'll come to tea with you tomorrow.'

So they did.

And that is the end of the story about how Teddy Robinson tried to keep up with the Joneses.

2

Teddy Robinson is Taken for a Ride

ONE day Teddy Robinson and Deborah went down to the sweetshop at the bottom of the road.

'Can I sit on the ledge outside and wait for you?' said Teddy Robinson. 'I like watching the people.'

'All right,' said Deborah, and she propped him up with his back to the window. Then she went in.

Teddy Robinson sat up very straight and proud, and thought how clever he was not to topple over. Soon a dog came sniffing round the door. It looked up at him and barked.

'Is that your shop?'

'No,' said Teddy Robinson, 'but that's my little girl inside. She's buying bull's-eyes.'

'Why do you look so proud if it's not your shop?' said the dog. 'Pride comes before a fall, you know.'

And at that minute Teddy Robinson toppled forward on his nose and fell over on to the pavement.

The dog ran off, thinking Teddy Robinson was after him, and for a while no one else saw what had happened. Then a lady came by and picked him up.

'Is that your pram?' she said, and popped him into a baby's pram close by. Then she walked on.

'No, it isn't,' said Teddy Robinson, 'but I'm glad she thought it was. It's a very nice pram.'

She propped him up with his back to the window.

Just then a lady hurried out of the shop, threw a magazine on top of him, looked at the baby asleep in the other end, and started to push the pram.

'Goodness gracious,' said Teddy Robinson under the magazine, 'I do believe I'm being carried away in front of my very eyes. What ever next?' And he wondered what Deborah would say.

After a while the pram stopped. The lady lifted the magazine off Teddy Robinson, and he saw that they were by a seat in the park. Then the lady saw him.

'Hallo, who ever put you in here?' she said.

Teddy Robinson couldn't tell her because he didn't know the name of the lady who had picked him up, so he looked friendly and said nothing.

The lady lifted him out and looked at him carefully. She saw that his fur was worn a little thin in places, and that one of his ears had once come off, and been sewn on again by hand. And she saw that his braces were fastened to his trousers with real buttons. But there wasn't a name tape anywhere.

'Someone cares for you, I can see that,' she said. And she sat him on the seat, hoping that whoever he belonged to would come and find him there.

When the lady had pushed the pram away, Teddy Robinson sat by himself, and thought how lucky he was to be a cared-for bear. And because it was pleasant in the park, and a bright sunny morning, he sang to himself to pass the time away,

> 'It's nice to be
> a cared-for bear –
> not one you pick up anywhere.
> My fur is wearing,
> here and there,
> but little signs
> of wear and tear
> will show in any well-loved bear.
> And Mummy,
> when she's time to spare,
> will always do a small repair.
> She even made
> the clothes I wear,

my dress, and trousers (just one pair),
each button sewn
with loving care –
I really am a lucky bear!'

Just then the park keeper came along. He stopped to pick up a newspaper that someone had dropped, then he saw Teddy Robinson on the seat.

'Well, I don't know!' he said, picking him up too. 'The things people leave lying about!'

'He can't mean me,' thought Teddy Robinson. 'I wasn't lying about. I was sitting up properly.'

The park keeper carried him and the newspaper along to a basket, which was fixed to a post by the side of the path. He put the newspaper in, then sat Teddy Robinson down on top of it. Then he went away.

Teddy Robinson sat inside the basket (which was made of wire and painted green) and felt very pleased.

'I think that man knew I was rather special,' he said to himself, 'so he's given me a seat all to myself. It's very nice, a splendid position. Most kind of him.'

After a while a cat came along. She stopped when she saw Teddy Robinson and walked all round the post, looking up at the basket and the notice on it. Then she sat down and stared.

Teddy Robinson bowed slightly, inside the basket, and said, 'Good day.'

'Miaou are you?' said the cat.

'Very well, thank you,' said Teddy Robinson.

"Miaou are you?"

'Is that your name?' said the cat, looking at the notice. 'Am I speaking to Mr Litter?'

'Oh, no. My name is Teddy Robinson.'

'Ow,' said the cat, in a miaouly sort of voice, 'And miaou are your kittens?'

'What kittens?' said Teddy Robinson.

'Isn't there a litter of kittens in that basket?'

'No, of course not,' said Teddy Robinson.

'Miaou?' said the cat. 'Ow very strange! That notice says LITTER HERE. But if you're not Mr Litter, and there isn't a litter of kittens in the basket, then that notice is all wrong.'

Teddy Robinson was quiet, thinking.

'Not that *I* care, I only wondered,' said the cat, and she stalked away, shaking the dust off her paws.

Then a big dog came bounding along. He stopped and sniffed round Teddy Robinson's feet.

'Don't do that,' said Teddy Robinson.

'Why not?' said the dog. 'I always sniff here.'

'It isn't for you. It's a cat's basket,' said Teddy Robinson.

'Oh, no, it's not!' said the dog. 'It's for waste-paper, and apple cores, and ice-cream cartons.'

'Rubbish,' said Teddy Robinson.

'That's right,' said the dog. 'That's why I like it. Fancy wanting to sit in a litter-bin!'

Just then a man came round the corner, whistling.

'That's my master,' said the dog. 'Look, he has just found a baby's glove. I bet you he'll put it in there with you. Cat's basket indeed!'

The man came up, carrying a little woollen glove. He looked at Teddy Robinson as if he was surprised to see him sitting there. Then he dropped the glove on to his lap, and walked on.

'I told you so!' barked the dog, and ran off after him.

'This was a nice little seat until I knew it was a rubbish basket,' thought Teddy Robinson sadly. 'Now I'm beginning to feel rather like rubbish myself.'

A bird flew down, perched on a near-by branch, and cocked its head cheekily at him.

'Is that your nest?' he chirped. 'It's just the place for you, isn't it?'

'No,' said Teddy Robinson, 'it's a rubbish basket.'

'And very nice too,' said the bird. 'I say, is that your glove? If so, I can tell you who's got the other one. She's just coming along now.'

At that minute a girl came round the corner, pushing a baby in a push-chair. The bird flew away.

The girl walked slowly, looking from side to side of the path as she went. Then she looked up and saw Teddy Robinson in the basket. She came over to him.

'Oh, look!' she said to the baby. 'There's a funny old teddy bear in here! And he's got your glove! He must have been looking after it for you. Oh, I am so glad we've found it!'

She lifted Teddy Robinson out of the basket.

'Poor old thing,' she said. 'You are a bit shabby, but it's a shame to throw you away.' And she put him in the push-chair with the baby.

'We must run now,' she said. 'We've been so long looking for that glove, Mummy will wonder where we are. And we haven't done the shopping yet.'

Then she began to run, and the push-chair began to rattle, and Teddy Robinson began to bounce, and the baby began to laugh. And they all went rattling and bouncing and bumping along at a great speed, out of the park and along the road.

*—rattling and bouncing and bumping along
at a great speed—*

Soon they came to a corner that Teddy Robinson knew. It was his own road! And a minute later they drew up outside the very shop where Deborah had left him.

Quickly the girl got out her purse and shopping bag, and lifted the baby down. She propped Teddy Robinson up on the window ledge while she put the push-chair against the wall.

Just then the baby toddled off into the shop by himself. The girl didn't wait to pick Teddy Robinson up, but ran after the baby as fast as she could.

Teddy Robinson was very glad to find himself back where he had started! Feeling muddled and happy, and rather pleased with his adventure, he began singing a muddled and happy little song.

'Here I are, just as I were,
sitting on the sill.
Who would say I'd been away?
(I'm still just sitting still.)

A lady took me for a ride
(she really didn't should),
I landed in a litter-bin
(I thought I'd gone for good).

But someone kindly pulled me out,
and home to here we ran,
so here I are, just as I were,
right back where I began!'

Then, who should he see but Deborah, running down the road towards him.

'Oh, there you are, Teddy Robinson!' she said, picking him up and hugging him. 'Do you know, I went all the way home without you! I *am* sorry I forgot you! What a dull time you must have had.'

'Oh, no!' said Teddy Robinson.

'You are a good boy just to sit and wait,' she said, 'but I suppose you couldn't really do anything else, could you?'

'Oh, couldn't I?' said Teddy Robinson. 'Shall I tell you a story about a teddy bear who got carried away in front of his very eyes, and a cat who thought his name was Litter, and a girl who was looking for a baby's glove?'

'Yes, tell me now,' said Deborah.

So Teddy Robinson told her the story all the way home.

And that is the end of the story about how
Teddy Robinson was taken for a ride.

3

Teddy Robinson and the Bird Cage

ONE day Teddy Robinson woke up from a nap and found that someone had put a bird cage beside him.

'Hallo!' he said. 'Is this for me?'

'No,' said Deborah, 'it's been left for Auntie Sue to fetch tomorrow. She is getting another bird.'

'I wish I was a bird,' said Teddy Robinson, and he thought what fun it would be to sit inside the fine gilt cage, flapping his wings, and singing to let every one know that spring had come.

'Can I sit inside?' he said.

'Not till I've asked Mummy,' said Deborah.

'Put me on top, then,' said Teddy Robinson.

So Deborah sat him on top of the bird cage and Teddy Robinson peered down through the bars and thought how cosy it looked inside. There were two little dishes for water and birdseed, and there was a tiny looking-glass for the bird to see itself in.

Teddy Robinson was just bending over to see if he could see himself in the looking-glass, when *crash* – he went tumbling down to the ground and bounced off the edge of the fender.

'It's a good thing it never hurts when teddy bears fall down,' he said, as Deborah picked him up.

'Sometimes my feelings get hurt, but never the rest of me. I'm glad I don't come up in bumps and bruises like you do.'

But a few minutes later something rather odd happened. Teddy Robinson looked at Deborah sideways, in a puzzled sort of way, and said, 'What ever have you done with your legs?'

Deborah looked down but could see nothing wrong, so she said, 'Nothing. What do you mean?'

'Well, you haven't got any!' said Teddy Robinson, looking surprised and beginning to laugh. 'And you

"What ever have you done with your legs?"

don't know how funny you look, just floating about on nothing!' And he laughed more and more every minute.

Deborah couldn't think why he was talking such nonsense. She came close to him and peered into his face. Then she said, 'Oh, Teddy Robinson, do you know what's happened? Your eye has cracked right across! And I suppose you can't see my legs because the lower half has dropped off. Here it is, in your lap. It must have happened when you fell off that bird cage.'

'Oh dear, that isn't funny at all!' said Teddy Robinson. 'You shouldn't laugh.'

'I wasn't laughing,' said Deborah. 'It was you.'

'Oh, yes, so it was,' said Teddy Robinson. 'Well, it did seem funny when it was only your legs that were missing, but my losing a glass eye is a very different thing. All the same, I'm glad it's only the lower half that's gone. I'd hate not to be able to see people's faces. I never was any good at telling what people were thinking by just looking at their feet.'

'We must ask Mummy to mend it,' said Deborah. 'You do look rather queer. I shouldn't like anyone to see you like this.' So they ran off to find Mummy.

Mummy found a tube of strong glue, and it wasn't long before she had stuck Teddy Robinson's eye together. But it still looked rather messy.

'Never mind, we can clean those smudges off when it is dry,' she said. 'But now you must be very careful not to move him. It will take a few hours for the glue to dry and stick hard. Until then he must stay quite still. Where shall we put him?'

'In the bird cage?' said Teddy Robinson.

'Yes, what a good idea!' said Mummy. 'Then we shan't forget, and pick him up without thinking.'

So Teddy Robinson was put in the bird cage and Mummy hung it up in the window. 'The air will help the glue to dry,' she said.

Teddy Robinson was very happy. He sat inside the cage and tried to make his arms flap up and down like wings, and sang twittery little bird songs,

> 'Look at me, oh, look at me!
> What a pretty bird I be!
> Up above the world so high,
> waiting for the glue to dry.'

Then, when his voice went gruff and growly with too much squeaking, he turned into a wild animal instead, and growled fiercely behind the bars.

Deborah was glad he was so happy, and not having to lie in bed until he was better.

'But you *are* making a lot of noise,' she said. 'You'll have to be quieter when Andrew comes, or we shan't be able to hear ourselves talk.'

'Oh dear, is Andrew coming?' said Teddy Robinson.

'Yes, you know he is. We asked him to tea.'

'Bother. I'd forgotten,' said Teddy Robinson. 'And is Spotty coming too?'

'I expect so, he usually does,' said Deborah.

"—tried to flap his arms up and down like wings—"

Spotty was Andrew's toy dog. Teddy Robinson didn't like him much because he always knew everything, and argued about everything, and made Teddy Robinson feel silly. He began growling again.

'Tell him I can't see him today.'

'That would be very rude,' said Deborah.

'But it's true,' said Teddy Robinson. 'I can't see him because my eye is smudgy with glue. I don't want him to see me either, not like this. Hide me.'

'But I can't, my poor boy,' said Deborah. 'You know I mustn't move you till your eye is stuck.'

Just then there was a ring at the door bell.

'Quick!' said Teddy Robinson. 'Hide me! Throw that tablecloth over the cage!'

Deborah just had time to climb up on the sill and cover the cage with the cloth before the door opened, and Andrew came in with Spotty.

'Hallo!' said Andrew, looking up at the bird cage hanging in the window. 'What have you got there?'

(Teddy Robinson sat very still, holding his breath.)

'It's a bird cage,' said Spotty. '*I* know that!'

'What have you got in it?' said Andrew to Deborah.

'A bird, of course,' said Spotty, before Deborah could answer. 'What would you expect to find in a bird cage, a hippopotamus?'

(Teddy Robinson began to laugh silently, and hoped he wasn't shaking the cage.)

Deborah pretended not to notice Spotty's rude way of talking, and Andrew walked all round, looking up at the cage from underneath.

'It is a fine one,' he said. 'You never told me you were getting a bird, Debbie. Is it new?'

'Of course it's new,' interrupted Spotty. 'It wasn't here last time. You do ask silly questions.'

'Be quiet, Spotty,' said Andrew. 'You're getting too cheeky.' (Teddy Robinson agreed silently, under the cloth.) 'Why have you put that cloth over it?' said Andrew to Deborah.

But before Deborah could say a word, Spotty interrupted again. 'Because the bird's asleep, of course.' (Teddy Robinson snored quickly.) 'Surely you knew they always cover a bird cage to keep it dark? Fancy not knowing that!'

'Well,' said Andrew, 'it's silly to stand here arguing about a bird that's asleep. Let's go and play outside. I'll leave Spotty in here with my coat.'

'Where's Teddy Robinson?' said Spotty, looking all round with his beady black eyes. 'Why isn't he here?'

'He's not very well today,' said Deborah.

'Where is he?' said Spotty.

'He's er – up above, resting,' said Deborah.

'What's the matter with him?' said Spotty.

'He had a little trouble with one of his eyes,' said Deborah, 'but he may be better before you go.'

'I'm sure he will,' said Spotty. 'He'll be all the better for seeing me. Can't he come down now?'

'Perhaps after tea,' said Deborah.

Then she and Andrew went off to play outside.

Spotty felt cross at being left alone on the sofa. He had been looking forward to showing off to someone, and now there was no one to show off to except a bird that was asleep. He began grumbling to himself.

'I didn't specially want to come out to tea anyway,' he said. 'Teddy Robinson isn't really clever enough for me. And now he's getting so old I suppose he's more or less falling to pieces. I expect that's why they've bought a bird instead. But fancy having a bird that has to sleep in the afternoon! That's not much company for an important guest like me.'

Teddy Robinson growled slightly under the cloth.

Spotty pricked up his ears, then he nodded to himself. 'That bird's snoring,' he said.

Teddy Robinson quickly changed his growling to little chirping noises, but his voice was husky after practising so much birdsong.

Spotty nodded again, solemnly. 'That bird's got a cold,' he said. 'I knew something was wrong with it.'

When Deborah and Andrew came back Spotty said, in an important voice, 'You know, there's something the matter with that bird of yours. I don't think it's much good. It's a little hoarse.'

'Oh, no, it isn't,' said Deborah, 'it's a teddy b . . .'

. . . there's something the matter with that bird

'A what?' said Spotty.

'A teddy bird,' said Deborah. 'I mean it's not a horse. It's just called Teddy.'

Spotty nodded, more solemnly still. 'Is he called Teddy after Teddy Robinson?' he said.

'Yes, I suppose he is,' said Deborah.

'Just as I thought,' said Spotty quickly. 'Poor old Teddy Robinson is falling to pieces, so they've gone and got a bird instead.' Then he said to Deborah, 'Does it know its name?'

'Oh, yes!' said Deborah.

'Teddy Bird!' called Spotty. 'Teddy Bird!'

(Teddy Robinson felt himself shaking with laughter, but he kept his mouth shut tightly and hoped the cage wasn't rocking.)

'That bird's deaf,' said Spotty. 'I knew there was something wrong with it. Hey, bird!'

'I heard,' said Teddy Robinson, in a high, twittery voice.

'Oh, so you're not deaf!' said Spotty. 'Birds should speak when they're spoken to. Or sing.'

Teddy Robinson began singing in his smallest voice, which had gone quavery with trying not to laugh out loud,

> 'Tweet, tweet, tweet,
>   snails are sweet to eat,
>   worms on toast I like the most,
>   and slugs are quite a treat.'

Spotty looked thoughtful. Then he said to Deborah

in a slow and important voice, 'There *is* something wrong with that bird. If you'll give me time to think, I may be able to tell you what it is.'

'Oh, no, please don't bother,' said Deborah.

'But it's no good you having a bird that's got something wrong with it,' said Spotty. 'Now if you'd take that cloth off, I'm sure I could spot what's wrong with it in a second.'

Teddy Robinson chirped loudly under the cloth, 'And anyone with half an eye could spot what's wrong with you. You know too much!'

Deborah said quickly, 'Thank you, Spotty, for being so interested, but it's our bird and we like it like that. Now, Andrew, shall we go and have tea? I heard Mummy ring the bell.'

Andrew took Spotty in to tea with him. He hoped it might take his mind off the bird.

When they were sitting down, Deborah said to Mummy, 'Do you think Teddy Robinson could come down after tea?'

'Oh, yes, I should think so,' said Mummy; 'I'll just go and see how he is.' And she got up and went out.

Deborah ran after her into the hall, and whispered quickly, 'Please put the cloth back over the cage. Andrew and Spotty think there's a real bird in there!' Then she ran back to the others.

When they all came back after tea, there was Teddy Robinson on the sofa. His eyes were bright and shiny and he looked very well indeed. (The crack where his eye had been broken didn't show at all.)

'Oh, so you're back?' said Spotty. 'How are you? I thought you were falling to pieces.'

'Me? I'm fine,' said Teddy Robinson, puffing out his chest. 'Never felt better. There's nothing I couldn't do. Why, I could fly over the wall and hit a potamus if there happened to be one there. How are you?'

'Very well, thank you,' said Spotty, still looking solemn. 'But I'm worried about that bird of yours. There's something wrong with it, and I can't quite put my paw on what it is.'

'I shouldn't worry,' said Teddy Robinson.

'Oh, but I do worry,' said Spotty. 'And now there's something else worrying me. You said just now that you could fly over the wall and hit a potamus. But you couldn't, you know. Shall I tell you why?'

'No, please don't,' said Teddy Robinson.

'I will, all the same,' said Spotty, in a heavy explaining sort of voice. 'You see, firstly you couldn't fly because you're not a bird. And secondly you couldn't hit a potamus because there isn't such a thing. Of course you might be able to hit a hippopotamus if you –'

'Oh, be quiet!' said Teddy Robinson. 'I can hitapotamus if I want to. I can hitapotato if I like. What's it got to do with you?'

Deborah had never heard Teddy Robinson so rude to anyone before. But secretly she was getting rather tired of Spotty too, so when Andrew said, 'I think I'll take him home now,' she said yes, perhaps it would be better.

Andrew looked up at the bird cage. 'I hope your bird *is* all right,' he said. 'It seems to have gone very quiet. Good-bye, and thank you for a nice tea.'

'Good-bye,' said Deborah and Teddy Robinson together, waving them off at the front door.

'*I* know what was wrong with that bird!' shouted Spotty, as Andrew carried him away. 'I said I'd be able to spot what was wrong with it if you only gave me time. That bird sang a song with words to it. Birds don't have words to their songs. I *said* it wasn't a proper bird!'

'Well, fancy that!' said Teddy Robinson to Deborah, when they'd gone. 'Spotty really is rather clever. I never thought of that!'

And that is the end of the story about
Teddy Robinson and the bird cage.

4

Teddy Robinson and the Sale

ONE day Teddy Robinson sat alone in the dining-room feeling rather dull. Soon he heard a ring at the door, then Mrs Grey's voice talking to Mummy.

'It's a lovely day for the sale,' she said. 'Are you and Deborah coming?'

'I am so sorry we can't,' said Mummy, 'but we have to go to town to do some shopping.'

'A sail!' said Teddy Robinson to himself. 'Now, fancy anyone going to town when they might be going for a sail!' And he thought how much he would like to be a sea-faring bear, with a sailor cap on his head and a coil of rope in his paws.

A little later Mummy came in, carrying two big vases, some cushions, a Japanese sunshade, and a pile of old clothes. She put them all on the table.

'What ever are those for?' said Deborah, coming in after her. 'Aren't we going to town?'

'Yes,' said Mummy, 'but these are for Mrs Grey. She said she would like them for the sale, so I've given her our key, and she's coming in to fetch them while we're out. Mrs White won't be coming to do the cleaning until later. Now do run and get ready.'

Teddy Robinson stared at all the things. 'Now, aren't people funny?' he thought. Why should Mrs

Grey want to take all that stuff for a sail? She's very
fond of flowers I know, but surely one vase would be
enough in a boat? And why take all those old clothes?
And why the Japanese sunshade?'

And then he suddenly had a wonderful idea. 'I
know!' he said. 'She's going a long way, a proper
voyage. She's probably sailing to Japan!'

He began thinking hard. 'I've always wanted to
travel. What a chance this would be, to go with kind
Mrs Grey! I suppose Mummy is taking Deborah to
town because she doesn't want her to go to Japan.
And Mummy can't go because Daddy would miss her.
But why shouldn't I go? I could always send Deborah
a card when I get there.' And he began singing,

> '*Yo-ho-ho* and *hip-hooray*!
> Here's a postcard just to say
> we landed in Japan today –
> lovely weather all the way –
> *yo-ho-ho* and *hip-hooray*!
> Love from me and Mrs Grey.'

Just then Deborah ran in to say good-bye. 'I hope
you won't be lonely,' she said, kissing him.

'Oh, no!' said Teddy Robinson, 'and I hope you
won't miss me. Just put me on the table, will you?'

So Deborah did. And when she and Mummy had
gone Teddy Robinson leaned back against the Japanese sunshade and thought about sailing to Japan.

'If I look the kind of chap who'd be handy on a
voyage, Mrs Grey may take me,' he said. He looked

down at his fat tummy. 'I may not be exactly ship-
shape but I'm sure I'm seaworthy.' And he pictured
himself very brown and brave and jolly, peering out
to sea with a paw shading his eyes, and shouting
'Land ahoy!' to Mrs Grey (who would be lying back
on the cushions, with the sunshade over her head).

> 'Land ahoy, dear Mrs Grey!
> I think we'll reach Japan today.
> Pray take my hairy, beary paw
> and let me help you step ashore.'

He was just thinking how well he would look,
standing with one brown furry paw in his braces, and
with the other delicately helping Mrs Grey ashore

he pictured himself peering out to sea

while Mrs Grey lay back on the cushions.

after their long voyage, when he heard the front door open, and then Mrs Grey herself came in.

She had another lady with her, a busy, bustling lady with a loud voice, who seemed to be in a great hurry, so Teddy Robinson decided not to mention the sail just yet. Instead he lay back and waited.

'You take the vases and the sunshade, Mrs Grey,' said the busy lady. 'I can manage this lot.' And she swept the cushions, the old clothes, and Teddy Robinson all together into her arms and marched out.

Teddy Robinson was thrown into the back of a car outside, with the cushions and old clothes on top of him. He heard the lady say, 'Put the vases on top; that's right. All aboard? Then off we go.' And a moment later they drove off.

'That's a very bossy lady,' said Teddy Robinson to himself, under the cushions. 'I hope she's not coming too.' He was cross with her for saying 'All aboard' because he'd been saving that up to say himself.

Soon the car stopped and the two ladies got out.

'Can we be at the sea already?' he thought. 'How quickly time goes when you're travelling!'

But they weren't at the sea. They were at the church hall. Teddy Robinson didn't know this because he was being carried inside among all the cushions and old clothes, and couldn't see anything. But soon, when he was uncovered, he was surprised to find himself lying on a long table. Mrs Grey was just walking away with the vases, and the bossy lady was standing over him sorting out the other things.

'This isn't worth anything. It can go in the jumble

lot,' she said, and pushed him down to the end of the table, beside a pile of old books.

Teddy Robinson lay on his back and looked around. On a shelf behind him, just above his head, stood a small china doll with bare shoulders and a very large skirt, shaped like a tea cosy. He stared up at her, trying not to squint, and said, 'Good afternoon, you're not coming for the sail, are you?'

The little doll looked down at him over her big skirt, with surprised, painted eyebrows.

'Of course I am,' she said. 'That's why I'm here. I had this dress made specially.'

Teddy Robinson looked at the dress, which was rose pink with tiny flowers worked on it.

'I was only thinking you're not very suitably dressed for a voyage,' he said.

'For a voyage?' said the doll. 'But who ever would want to go in a boat in a beautiful dress like mine? It was made specially for this sale of work. I'm a tea cosy. What are you?'

'Oh dear,' said Teddy Robinson, all in a muddle, 'I hardly know what I am now! If this is a sale of work, and you're a tea cosy, I must be a great big silly mistake who oughtn't to be here at all.' And he felt awfully silly to be lying there in his old trousers and braces, not even in his best purple dress.

'I do beg your pardon,' he said. 'I see it's me who's not very suitably dressed. I have got a best dress at home, but I thought I was going in a boat.'

'Never mind,' said the little doll, in a soft tea cosy voice, 'I expect someone will buy you.'

'Oh dear!' said Teddy Robinson. 'Are we going to be bought?'

'Of course,' said the doll. 'That's what a sale of work is. People make things for it, then other people come and buy them. Didn't you see my label? It says HANDMADE – TWO POUNDS.'

Teddy Robinson felt more awkward than ever. 'But I'm not handmade,' he said, 'and I'm quite old.'

'Yes, I can see that,' said the cosy doll. 'That's why you're in the jumble lot. But never mind, you'll make a nice present for someone.'

Teddy Robinson was quiet for a minute, thinking. Then he said, in a light sort of voice, 'I suppose there isn't a label on me, is there? I don't feel one pinned on. Not that it matters – I just wondered.'

'No, not one for you specially,' said the cosy doll. 'There is a card which says ANYTHING 2p just behind you, but I wouldn't worry about that.'

'Oh, no,' said Teddy Robinson. 'I wouldn't. After all, I'm not *anything*. I'm me.'

But he did worry a little. 'Who can say how much I'm worth?' he thought. 'Deborah would say at least a hundred pounds, but that bossy lady didn't think I was worth anything. I don't *feel* worth a penny just now, but that's because I'm disappointed, and I'm in the wrong place. I wish I wasn't here. My place is at home with Deborah. It serves me right for wanting to go to Japan without her.'

Then he suddenly felt better. 'That doll said I'd make a nice present for someone,' he said. 'If I'm

"I suppose there isn't a label on me, is there?"

going to be a present I needn't worry at all. After all, it's the thought that counts.'

'Oh, look!' said a lady's voice above his head. 'Wouldn't that make a perfect present for Aunt Jane?'

Teddy Robinson smiled and tried not to look too proud. Then he heard a rustle of paper, and a moment later he saw that the tea cosy doll had gone.

'They must have wrapped her up by mistake instead of me,' he said to himself, and he felt sorry for the lady's Aunt Jane, who was only going to get a tea cosy for a present instead of a teddy bear.

'Never mind, it leaves all the more of me for some-one else,' he thought, and waited patiently.

But nobody noticed him after that for quite a long time. He missed the kind tea cosy doll and felt sad to think he would never see her again.

Then along came a little lady in a brown coat, with a big black shopping bag. She was talking to herself as she looked at all the price labels.

'There, now,' she said, 'it isn't a proper jumble sale at all! It's a sale of work. Much too dear for me. Fancy me making such a silly mistake!'

Teddy Robinson was glad to think someone else had made a silly mistake too. He hoped she would see him. And she did. She read the notice which said ANYTHING 2p and then, before he even had time to say 'Good afternoon,' he found himself being pushed down into the bottom of her big black shopping bag.

An apron, a pair of slippers, and a pound of onions were there already, and it was very dark.

Then the little lady in the brown coat, and Teddy Robinson in the black bag (with the apron, and the slippers, and the onions), all went bobbing along together, out of the hall and away down the road.

'Oh dear,' said Teddy Robinson, 'this is very different from sailing to Japan! Though it does feel rather like a rough sea. But a shopping bag doesn't make much of a boat, and the sea breeze smells of onions. I wish I hadn't come.'

Then he suddenly realized he didn't know where he was going either. 'And I thought I was going to be a present!' he said. 'But if so, I ought to be wrapped up nicely and tied with ribbon. If I'm going to be a nice surprise I ought to look like one. Oh dear, I do wish I knew where I was going!'

They stopped at last. Teddy Robinson heard the sound of a door being knocked on, and the handle turned as it was opened. Then he heard the little lady say, 'Hallo, Lily! I just popped in on my way back. If you're ready we can go home together.'

And he heard the person called Lily say, 'Why, Flo, how nice! Come in, I've nearly finished.'

Then Teddy Robinson, still in the bag (with the apron, and the slippers, and the onions), heard the chink of teacups, and the two ladies talking. The little lady told her friend all about the sale, and how she'd bought a funny old teddy for two pence.

'He's not much to look at,' she said, 'but he's got a nice old face, the sort a child likes.'

Teddy Robinson nearly felt cross when he heard this, then he remembered he had thought just the same about the little lady when he first saw her. So he decided to go on feeling friendly after all.

'And I'd have bought *her* for two pence if she'd been for sale,' he said kindly. 'But I'm sure I wouldn't have left her in the bottom of a bag with a whole lot of onions. I do wish she'd let me out!'

And then, all of a sudden, a most surprising thing happened. He heard a door open, and *Deborah*'s voice saying, 'Oh, *please*, have you seen my teddy anywhere? I've lost him!' (and she sounded so sad). He felt dizzy with surprise!

Then everything seemed to happen at once. Lily

said no, she hadn't seen him, and the little lady said, 'Never mind, dear. See if you like this instead.' Then the big black shopping bag was turned upside down, and Teddy Robinson (and the apron, and the slippers, and the onions), came tumbling out on to the table. And Teddy Robinson saw that he was in his very own kitchen!

There was Mrs White, who came to help with the cleaning (she was the lady called Lily!). And there was the little lady in the brown coat (she was Mrs White's friend, Flo, whom he hadn't met before). And there was his own dear Deborah, so glad to see him that she thought she would never stop hugging him!

— came tumbling out on to the table.

'Am I a nice surprise?' said Teddy Robinson, very surprised himself.

'Oh, yes, the nicest I ever had!' said Deborah.

Then everyone started talking, and explaining, and laughing, and being surprised, all together.

'Have you ever been sold?' said Teddy Robinson later, as Deborah carried him happily up to bed. 'I have. I went for a sail in a boat that wasn't there, and I got sold instead. But it's awfully jolly to be sold to someone new, and then come back as a nice surprise to your own funny old family!'

And that is nearly, but not quite, the end of the story. The real end came two days later when a parcel came for Mummy, from a grown-up niece. And inside was the rose-pink tea cosy doll. Teddy Robinson was so pleased to see her. He had quite forgotten that Mummy's real name was Jane!

And that is the end of the story about
Teddy Robinson and the sale.

5

Teddy Robinson and the Caravan

ONE day Teddy Robinson set off for a holiday in a caravan. He was so excited that he sang songs and asked questions all the way there.

'Is it a gipsy caravan?' he said. 'Will it have a horse? Shall we be gipsies and follow the fair? Bless my braces, that's the life for a bear like me!'

But Daddy said, 'No, it's a holiday caravan. It's a new one, and it lives behind a farm.'

'I shall be a gipsy, all the same,' said Teddy Robinson, 'a gipsy bear with the wind in my hair –'

'You can't,' said Deborah. 'It's fur.'

'I know, but it doesn't rhyme,' said Teddy Robinson, and he sang loudly,

> 'A bear doesn't care
> if it's fur or hair,
> as long as he's out in the open air.
> I'll follow the fair,
> so there, so there,
> I'll still be a jolly old gipsy bear!'

But he forgot all about being a gipsy when he saw the caravan. It was so full of surprises.

First Mummy lifted a flap from the wall, and it turned into a table.

'Well, fancy that!' said Teddy Robinson.

Then Deborah pulled out a partition from inside the wardrobe door, and it turned into a wall that made the caravan into two rooms.

'Well, I never!' said Teddy Robinson.

Then Daddy turned a key in another wall and said, 'Now look at this!' And the whole wall came outwards, and there inside was a big bed standing on its head, all ready to be let down.

'Well, bless my braces!' said Teddy Robinson. 'If beds can come out of walls, and walls can come out of wardrobes, anything can happen. Elephants can come out of bird cages, and teddy bears can come out of teapots.' And he got so excited that he fell over backwards and landed in the big teapot that Mummy had just put on the table.

'Why, so they can!' said Daddy, and he put the lid on top of his head. 'Now sing us a song!'

Teddy Robinson looked around at the things Mummy was laying out for tea, and sang,

> 'Veal and ham,
> bread and jam,
> what a lucky bear I am!
> Cake I see,
> and eggs for tea,
> what a lucky bear I be!
> (but please don't pour the tea on me).'

'All right,' said Mummy, laughing, 'but get out quickly. I'm just going to make it. And then we must unpack and make up the beds.'

"Veal and ham, bread and jam, what a lucky bear I am!"

After tea Teddy Robinson and Deborah ran around the fields until Mummy called them in to bed.

Soon they were tucked up on the seat under the window (which was now a cosy bed), enjoying all the bumps and bangs, as Daddy pulled out the partition and let down the big bed from the wall. Every time Mummy opened a locker, or Daddy fetched a water can, there was a great bumping and banging and clattering, and the whole caravan shook.

It wasn't a bit like going to bed at home.

Teddy Robinson sang a noisy little lullaby,

> 'Down comes the bed,
> *bumpety-bump*,
> out comes the wall,
> *thumpety-thump*,
> *clatter-and-clang*
> go bucket and can,

we're going to sleep
in a caravan!'

and he sang *biffety-bang*, *bumpety-bump*, *clattery-
clang*, *thumpety-thump*, until Deborah fell asleep.

When at last everything was quiet and even Daddy
and Mummy were asleep, he lay with his eyes wide
open, staring at the sky through the open window,
and listening to the country sounds. Corn rustled in
the field, far away a dog barked, and a cow coughed
in a field close by. Then he too fell asleep.

Once he half woke, hearing rustlings and scratchings
quite near, and tiny voices squeaking. And once there
was a harsh, shrill cry and he woke with a jump,
feeling his fur stand up on end with fright. But
Deborah slept on, so he went to sleep again too, and
in the morning he had forgotten all about it.

Everything was a muddle in the morning. There
were beds to make, blankets to fold, and breakfast
to cook, all at the same time, and no room for anything. Teddy Robinson simply didn't know where he
was.

First Daddy tripped over him on the floor, and
popped him into a locker. Then Mummy threw
blankets in on top and nearly smothered him. Then
Deborah found him and put him in the big bed, but
Daddy came and pushed it up into the wall, and
turned the key.

By the time he was found again he was very
grumpy, and all he would say was, 'Let me out!
Let me out!'

'But you are out,' said Deborah.

'No, right out,' said Teddy Robinson. 'I've been locked in a locker, and folded in a bed (upside down inside a wall, and standing on my head), I'd rather be a gipsy bear and live outside instead.'

'All right, let's go to the farm,' said Deborah.

'Will there be cows?' said Teddy Robinson.

'Oh, yes,' said Deborah, 'chickens too.'

'I don't think I will,' he said. 'Not that I'm *frightened* of cows, but I don't want to catch a cold. I heard one of those cows coughing last night.'

'You stay in bed then,' said Deborah.

But Teddy Robinson still had a picture in his mind of being a gipsy bear, living out of doors, perhaps with a little camp fire to cook on.

He began mumbling to himself, in his own round-and-round sort of way, 'I may be only a teddy bear, but I'm not a stay-in-beddy bear, I'm a jolly, rough-and-ready bear, I'd rather live in the open air, shutting me up just isn't fair, I'd *rather* be an outdoor bear, a carefree, open-airy bear, without a worry without a care, not even any clothes to wear . . .'

'Oh, all right,' said Deborah, 'but I won't have you sitting about with no clothes on. People will say I don't look after you properly. Anyway I thought you were afraid of catching cold?'

'Oh, yes, so I am!' said Teddy Robinson, 'but the fresh air will soon cure that.'

So half an hour later he was sitting on a grassy bank under the hedge, wearing his trousers and a red-

and-white-spotted handkerchief round his neck. Beside him was a bundle of twigs, laid like a fire, and, best of all, on top of the twigs was an old tin kettle that Deborah had found in the ditch.

'You can have this for your own,' she said, then she kissed him good-bye and ran off to the farm.

Teddy Robinson was very happy now. 'This is the life for me,' he said. 'I feel better already. Fresh air and exercise, that's the thing. I can do without the exercise but I do like plenty of fresh air.' And he took deep breaths, sitting up very straight with his tummy sticking out.

A fieldmouse ran past, looked up at him sideways, and disappeared over the bank. He sat very still and hoped she would come back. Soon she did. She came backwards and forwards many times, and at last she stopped, with her whiskers twitching.

'Good morning,' said Teddy Robinson. 'This is a fine life, isn't it?'

'It may be for you,' said the fieldmouse rather sharply. 'Camping is all very well for a city gentleman on his own, but it's very different with a family to feed. So much fetching and carrying!'

'Dear me, I'm sorry,' said Teddy Robinson, trying not to look so happy.

'It was easier when we lived in the cornfield,' she said. 'But now we live under a house – a very *nice* house, with very nice people – (we always choose very nice people) – it's just behind you.'

'Oh, you mean our caravan!' said Teddy Robin-

"This is a fine life, isn't it?"

son, very pleased. 'But why do you live under us when you could live out in the cornfield?'

The fieldmouse shivered. 'Haven't you heard?' she whispered. 'Haven't you heard – in the night?'

Teddy Robinson suddenly remembered. 'I did hear rustlings,' he said. 'Was that you? But you were squeaking as if you were frightened.' Then he remembered the harsh, shrill scream. 'What was it?' he asked, and his fur tingled as he remembered.

'It was Hooo-hooo, the owl,' she said, in the smallest trembling whisper. 'He's terrible. He hunts us in the night, flying over the fields and calling *Who-o-o? Who-o-o?* He means us, of course, and we all lie trembling in our beds. My children have such lovely bright eyes! He sees them shining in the moonlight, and then he swoops. That's why we're living under your house. Please don't tell!'

'Of course I won't,' said Teddy Robinson.

When Deborah fetched him in at tea time she was so full of the farm she could talk of nothing else.

'This holiday is doing you good,' said Mummy, looking at her. 'I do believe you're fatter and browner, and your eyes are brighter already.'

'Thank you,' said Teddy Robinson, bowing.

'Yes, you too,' said Mummy. 'It must be all that fresh air. I hope every day is as nice.'

It was. Every day the sun shone. So every morning Deborah ran off to the farm, and Teddy Robinson sat in his own little camp on top of the bank, with his unlit fire and his old tin kettle.

His new friend, the fieldmouse (whom no one else knew about yet), soon became his old friend. And every day Teddy Robinson seemed to get fatter and browner, and his eyes seemed to shine more brightly.

Only at night, when he heard the scream of Hooo-hooo, the owl, he snuggled down in bed with Deborah and was glad he wasn't still camping out.

Then one day, near the end of the holiday, Daddy said the caravan was going to be moved nearer the farm for a while. Teddy Robinson ate no breakfast at all, he was so worried at this dreadful news.

As soon as he could, he told Mrs Fieldmouse.

'Oh! What ever shall I do?' she squeaked. 'With no roof over our heads where should we be?'

'You'd still be in the field,' said Teddy Robinson.

'But I've an idea. Why don't you all move into my camp? The kettle would make a nice nest for you, and Hooo-hooo would never find you there.'

'Oh, Mr Robinson Bear, how kind of you!' she cried. 'What should I do without you? I'm sure we shall be most comfortable in your cosy kettle.'

'But you must move quickly,' he said. 'The caravan is being towed away first thing tomorrow.'

'Oh dear!' said Mrs Fieldmouse, 'but it will take me all night to move my babies, one at a time. And I've only got two pairs of paws.' She stared hard at Teddy Robinson. 'Now you've got two fine, strong brown arms, Mr Robinson Bear. I wonder . . .'

'Oh, but I couldn't!' said Teddy Robinson. 'My arms are all right, but I'm no good on my legs.'

He tried to picture himself crawling about under the caravan, carrying away the baby fieldmice, but he knew it was impossible, and he felt ashamed.

Mrs Fieldmouse said, sniffing a little, 'I'd have thought a big, strong gentleman like you (who's looking all the better for his holiday) would have been only too glad to help a poor, homeless family. Or don't city gentlemen care for children?'

'Oh, it's not that!' said poor Teddy Robinson. 'I love babies, truly I do.'

Then he suddenly had an idea. 'Mrs Fieldmouse,' he said, sitting up straight and proud like a soldier, 'you said the children's eyes shine brightly in the moonlight, and that's how Hooo-hooo sees them. Well, my eyes shine brightly too. And I'm much

He tried to picture himself crawling about under the caravan,

but he knew it was impossible.

bigger. I myself will keep an eye open for him. I'll ask if I can stay out tonight. Just leave it to me.'

'Oh, dear bear!' cried Mrs Fieldmouse. 'What a good friend you are! Dear me! What ever shall I do when you've gone!' and she wiped away a tear.

'I'll be back,' said Teddy Robinson. 'I'll ask Deborah to bring me again before we go home.'

'Oh, no! It's good-bye for ever, I know it is!' she cried, and she made tiny sniffling noises.

'Don't cry,' said Teddy Robinson bravely. 'I will come back if I don't get eaten. I hope I don't even more than you do.'

Deborah wasn't at all sure whether she ought to

leave Teddy Robinson out all night – not on purpose.
But in the end she let him have his way.

So at bedtime, there he was, sitting all by himself
up on the roof, waiting for it to get dark.

He heard first Deborah, then Mummy and Daddy
go to bed. He listened to all the jolly bumps and bangs
and clatters going on inside the caravan as usual, and
wished he was down there too, safely tucked up with
Deborah. Then he saw the farm lights go out and
everything was quiet.

Soon the moon rose. Teddy Robinson waited with
both eyes open, and, to keep his spirits up, sang a
Brave Song,

> 'Hooo, Ha, Hooo,
>   I'm not afraid of you.
>   I know the terrible things you do,
>   you wicked old owl, *yahoo, yahoo,*
>   but I'm still not afraid of you, Hooo-hooo,
>   I'm still not afraid of you.'

(but he was, of course).

Then in the distance, he heard a faint *Who-o,
Who-o,* and the sound of large wings coming nearer.
He felt as if he were frozen to the roof, and the fur on
his ears stood up on end with fright.

With a great rustle of leaves, the owl landed in the
top of a tree. '*Who-o-o?*' he called, in a horrible
harsh scream. '*Who-o-o?*'

Teddy Robinson sat tight, his eyes shining brightly,
and drew a big, brave breath. Then, as Hooo-hooo

swooped down towards him, he shouted out at the top of his voice, 'You! You! You!'

The owl swerved sideways with surprise. 'Who-o are you?' he said, with a short, quavery squawk.

'I'm an owl-eater!' shouted Teddy Robinson. 'And I've been keeping an eye open for you!'

'Who?' squawked the owl faintly.

'Why, you! You! You silly old owl,' said Teddy Robinson. 'Be off before I eat you for my supper!'

'Ooo!' said the owl. And he circled round with a great flapping of wings and flew away.

It was nearly dawn when Teddy Robinson heard squeakings in the hedge, and knew that Mrs Field-mouse had safely moved her family. He sighed with relief.

the fur on his ears
stood up on end with fright.

He thought of all the babies being put to bed in his kettle, squeaking with excitement at moving in the night. He pictured them snuggling down together in their little brown fur coats. The thought made him drowsy. In another minute he was asleep.

When Deborah fetched him down in the morning, his fur was all wet with dew. He was longing to tell her all about Mrs Fieldmouse and the owl, but already the men had come to move the caravan.

As it was towed away across the field, he stared hard out of the back window, towards his little camp. He hoped Mrs Fieldmouse was watching, but it was too far away for him to see. He felt sad. His holiday was nearly over and he might never see her again.

Much later on, he was still sitting humped up by himself, when Deborah ran in, shouting, 'Oh, Teddy Robinson! Guess what!' She hugged him till he squeaked. 'Daddy's bought the caravan for our very own! We can come back here every summer!'

Teddy Robinson was pleased! He had to explore the caravan all over again then, because somehow it seemed different now he knew it was their own. And it looked nicer than ever!

Teddy Robinson did go to his little camp again. Deborah took him before they went home. He was afraid anyone so big might frighten the fieldmice, so he said, 'Leave me alone a minute, and I promise I'll tell you all about it on the way home.' So she did.

Teddy Robinson blew down the kettle spout and it made a hollow, roaring noise. He heard tiny scufflings down below, then a frightened bright eye gleamed up at him through the darkness.

'Hallo, Mrs Fieldmouse, are you there?' he said.

'Oh, Mr Robinson, dear bear, it's you!' squeaked Mrs Fieldmouse. 'Oh, welcome to Cosy Kettle! Look, dear children, come and see who's here. It's our dear friend, Mr Robinson Bear!'

Teddy Robinson was pleased at such a welcome.

'I told you I'd come back!' he roared happily down the spout. 'And what's more I'm coming back next summer, and the summer after, and the summer after that, and every summer for ever and ever hooray!'

And he got so excited, thinking about all the lovely summers to come, that he forgot he was on the edge of the bank and tumbled forward on his nose, and rolled head over heels all the way down to the bottom, where Deborah was waiting for him.

And that is the end of the story about
Teddy Robinson and the caravan.

6

Teddy Robinson and the Teddy-Bear Brooch

ONE day a letter came for Deborah and Teddy Robinson. It was from Auntie Sue, and it said:

DEAR DEBORAH AND TEDDY ROBINSON,

Please tell Mummy I shall be coming to tea with you all tomorrow. I hope you will like the little brooch.

And pinned to a card inside the letter was a dear little teddy-bear brooch. It was pink with silver eyes, and Deborah thought it was very beautiful. She gave the letter to Mummy to read and pinned the brooch on the front of her dress.

'Wasn't there anything for me?' asked Teddy Robinson. Deborah looked inside the envelope again.

'No,' she said, 'there's nothing else.'

'Oh,' said Teddy Robinson. 'Then can I have the envelope? It will make me a soldier's hat.'

So Deborah put the envelope on his head. Then

Teddy Robinson said, 'Fetch me the wooden horse, please. It's time I went on duty. I'm going to guard the palace.'

So Deborah fetched the wooden horse.

'And I want a sentry-box, please,' said Teddy Robinson.

'I haven't got a sentry-box,' said Deborah. 'Will the toy-box do?'

"Do you really _like_ it in there?"

'Yes, if you stand it up on end,' said Teddy Robinson.

So Deborah emptied the toy-box and stood it up on end. Then she put the wooden horse inside, and Teddy Robinson sat on its back with the envelope on his head. He didn't really feel like playing soldiers at all, but he wanted to sit somewhere quietly and not be talked to for a while.

'Do you really *like* it in there?' asked Deborah, peeping in at him.

'Yes, thank you,' said Teddy Robinson, 'but you mustn't talk to me. I'm on duty.'

"Fancy her sending a brooch with a bear!"

So Deborah went off to play by herself, and Teddy
Robinson sat on the wooden horse and began thinking about why he was feeling so quiet. He knew it was
something to do with the teddy-bear brooch.

He began mumbling to himself in a gentle,
grumbling growl:

> '*Fancy* her sending a brooch with a bear!
> It isn't polite and it isn't fair.
> There's a bear here already
> who lives in the house.
> Why *couldn't* she send her a brooch with a mouse?
> Or a brooch with a dog?
> Or a brooch with a cat?
> Nobody'd *ever* feel hurt at that.
> But a brooch with a bear
> isn't fair
> on the bear
> who lives in the house,
> and who's *always* been there.'

Teddy Robinson went on mumbling to himself and
getting more and more grumbly and growly. He was
feeling very cross with Auntie Sue, so he said all the
nasty things he could think of, for quite a long while.
Then he ended up by saying:

> 'When *she* gets a present I only hope
> that all *she* gets is an envelope.'

After that he began to feel quite sorry for Auntie
Sue, and much better himself.

He heard Mummy come out into the garden and

say to Deborah, 'Hallo! Why ever have you emptied the toy-box and stood it up on end like that?'

And he heard Deborah say, 'Hush! Teddy Robinson's inside. He says he's guarding the palace, but I think he's sad about something.'

'Oh, well,' said Mummy, 'bring him with you. I was going to ask if you would like to help make a fruit jelly for Auntie Sue tomorrow.'

'Oh, yes,' said Deborah. 'Teddy Robinson can sit on the kitchen table and watch. He always likes that.'

She bent down and peeped inside the toy-box.

'Have you finished guarding the palace yet, Teddy Robinson?'

'Yes, I'm just coming off duty this minute,' said Teddy Robinson. 'Help me down.'

Deborah helped him down, and together they went into the kitchen. Mummy had poured some pink jelly into a bowl, and she gave Deborah some cherries and slices of banana on a plate.

'Drop them into the jelly, one at a time,' said Mummy. 'It's still rather soft and runny, but to-morrow it will be set beautifully, with the fruit inside it.'

So Deborah knelt on a chair and dropped the pieces of fruit carefully into the bowl, and Teddy Robinson sat on the kitchen table and said 'Plop' every time she dropped a cherry in, and 'Bang' every time she dropped a slice of banana in. He always liked helping when Deborah was working with Mummy in the kitchen.

He looked down into the bowl

Every time Deborah leaned forward to look in the bowl, Teddy Robinson saw the teddy-bear brooch on her dress, its silver eyes shining and winking in the sunlight. He tried not to look, because he didn't want to feel cross again; but it was so pretty it was difficult not to notice it.

And then Teddy Robinson saw that the pin of the brooch had come undone, and every time Deborah moved it was sliding a little way farther out of her dress. He held his breath, waiting to see what would happen, and a moment later it slipped out and fell with a gentle *plop* right into the middle of the jelly-bowl!

Deborah was saying something to Mummy at the

minute, so she did not notice. Teddy Robinson wondered if he ought to tell her, but it seemed a pity to remind her about it.

'After all, she's still got me,' he said to himself. 'She didn't really need another teddy bear.'

He looked down into the bowl, but there was no sign of the teddy-bear brooch. If it was there it was well hidden among all the cherries and banana slices. Teddy Robinson was glad to think it had gone.

Deborah dropped the last slice of banana into the bowl.

'There,' she said, 'it's all finished. You forgot to say "Bang," Teddy Robinson.'

'Bang,' said Teddy Robinson. 'Do you feel as if you'd lost something?'

'No,' said Deborah. 'Do you?'

'No,' said Teddy Robinson. 'At least, if I have I'm glad I've lost it.'

'You *are* a funny boy,' said Deborah. 'I don't know what you're talking about.'

Teddy Robinson began to feel very jolly now that the teddy-bear brooch had gone. He kept singing funny little songs, and asking Deborah silly riddles, and making her laugh, so that it wasn't until after tea that she suddenly noticed she had lost it.

'Oh dear! Where ever can it be?' she said. 'It must have fallen off while we were playing. Help me look for it, Teddy Robinson.'

So Teddy Robinson and Deborah looked under chairs and under tables and all through the toy cupboard, but, of course, they couldn't find it anywhere.

Teddy Robinson began to sing:

> 'Oh, where, oh, where
> is the Broochy Bear?
> First look here,
> and then look there.
> *I* can't see him anywhere.
> He's lost! He's lost! The Broochy Bear!'

'You sound as if you're *glad* he's lost,' said Deborah. 'Why are you so jolly?'

'Because I'm jolly sorry,' said Teddy Robinson.

'Oh, don't be so silly,' said Deborah. 'Let's go and ask Mummy.'

But Mummy hadn't seen the teddy-bear brooch

They couldn't find it anywhere.

anywhere either. 'He must be somewhere about,' she said. 'You'll just have to go on looking.'

'But we've looked everywhere – haven't we, Teddy Robinson?'

'Well, we haven't looked *everywhere*,' he said, 'because we haven't looked on top of the roof, or under the floor, or up the chimney, but we did look in quite a lot of places.'

'But I haven't been on top of the roof, or under the floor, or up the chimney,' said Deborah.

'No,' said Teddy Robinson, 'but you haven't been in the jelly either.'

'What *are* you talking about?' said Deborah. 'And why *are* you so jolly? I don't see anything to feel so happy about.'

The next day Auntie Sue came at tea-time, as she had promised. She was very pleased to see everybody, and because she was his friend as well, Teddy Robinson was allowed to sit up at the table. He had a chair with three cushions on it, so he was high enough to have quite a nice view of everything.

There were sandwiches and cakes and chocolate biscuits, and in the middle of the table was the fruit jelly. It had set beautifully, and Mummy had turned it out on to a glass dish.

Deborah pointed it out to Auntie Sue.

''Teddy Robinson and I helped to make that,' she said.

'Did you really?' said Auntie Sue. 'How very clever of you both!'

She turned to smile at them, and then she said:

'Why isn't Teddy Robinson wearing his brooch? Didn't he like it?'

'Oh!' said Deborah. 'Was it for him? How dreadful! I thought it was for me, and I pinned it on the front of my dress, and now I've lost it. I can't think where it is.'

'It's sure to turn up soon,' said Mummy. 'We know it's somewhere in the house.' Then she and Auntie Sue started talking together about grown-up things.

'Never mind, Teddy Robinson,' whispered Deborah. 'I'm sure we shall find him again soon.'

'The trouble is he mayn't be there any more to find,' said Teddy Robinson.

'Where?' asked Deborah.

'Where he was yesterday when we couldn't find him,' said Teddy Robinson. 'I'm afraid he may have melted.'

'What ever do you mean?' said Deborah. 'Do you know where he is? If you do I wish you'd tell me.'

'Well,' said Teddy Robinson, 'think of something round and pink, with a lot of banana in it, that's on the table, and when you've guessed what I mean I'll tell you.'

'Something round and pink with a lot of banana in it?' said Deborah. 'Can you mean the jelly?'

'Yes,' said Teddy Robinson. 'Don't look now, but I *think* the teddy-bear brooch is inside that.'

"Think of something round and pink"

'Good gracious!' said Deborah. 'How ever did that happen?'

'He fell out of your dress when you were dropping the fruit in,' said Teddy Robinson. 'I saw the pin was undone and I didn't tell you, because I wanted you to lose him.'

'But why?' asked Deborah.

'Because you'd already got me, and I didn't think you needed another bear,' said Teddy Robinson.

'Oh, you silly boy!' said Deborah. 'How could you think I'd ever love a silly little teddy bear on a brooch as much as I love you?'

Teddy Robinson was very pleased to hear Deborah say this.

'But you mustn't call him silly,' he said. 'He's mine now, and he's really rather special. I do hope he hasn't melted. Ask Mummy to start serving the jelly, then perhaps we'll find him.'

So Mummy began to serve the jelly, and a moment later what should she find but the little teddy-bear brooch, all among the cherries and slices of banana! She was very surprised.

'How ever did he get there?' she said.

'He fell in when I was dropping the fruit in,' said Deborah. 'Teddy Robinson has just told me so.'

'Well, fancy that!' said Auntie Sue. 'So he can have his brooch after all.'

Then they washed the teddy-bear brooch, and dried him, and he was pinned on to Teddy Robinson's trouser-strap; and Teddy Robinson said 'Thank you' to Auntie Sue for such a nice present. He was very pleased, because the teddy-bear brooch looked as good as new. He hadn't melted a bit, and his silver eyes still sparkled and shone, just as if he'd never been inside a jelly at all.

*And that is the end of the story about
Teddy Robinson and the teddy-bear brooch.*

7

Teddy Robinson and the Fairies

ONCE upon a time Teddy Robinson and Deborah went to stay for a few days with Auntie Sue in her cottage in the country.

They had a lovely time. All day long the bees buzzed in the garden and the cows mooed in the fields, and every evening Auntie Sue read them a fairy story out of a book that she used to enjoy when she was a little girl. So they went to sleep every night with their heads full of fairy stories and country things.

One afternoon Teddy Robinson said to Deborah, 'I like it here. The flowers are full of honey, and the woods smell like hot blackberry jam. It's no wonder fairies choose to live in the country. Do you think we shall see any fairies while we are here?'

And Deborah said, 'I don't know, Teddy Robinson; but you've just given me a good idea. Let's go out now, all by ourselves, and see if we can find some!'

So they set off together down the lane.

Soon they came to a place where white flowers with long, twisted stalks were growing all over the hedge.

'I think a crown of those would suit me,' said Deborah, and she pulled down a long string of the

*Deborah made a
garland for each of them.*

flowers and began to twist them into a garland to
wear round her head.

'Yes,' said Teddy Robinson. 'I think they might
suit me as well, don't you? Or should I look soppy?'

'No, they would suit you very well,' said Deborah.
'We shall look a bit more like fairies ourselves if we
wear garlands of flowers. They all do in Auntie Sue's
fairy book. Sit still and let me fit you.'

So Teddy Robinson sat still and watched while
Deborah made a garland for each of them, and fitted
them on their heads. Then they set off down the lane
again.

A little farther on they came to a turning where a
narrow grassy path led off between trees and bushes,
and disappeared among the leaves. The trees met

overhead like an archway, so that it all looked very green and quiet and secret.

'Oh, look!' said Deborah. 'That is *just* the sort of place where fairies would live. It looks almost magic.'

So very quietly they went down the little green lane, peeping here and peeping there, under leaves and into bushes, and up into the branches over their heads.

But not a sign of a fairy did they see.

'I'm sure if there *are* any fairies they would be here,' said Deborah, after they had been looking for quite a long while. 'I wonder why we can't find any.'

... down the little green lane.

'Perhaps we are looking too hard,' said Teddy Robinson. 'Don't you think if we just sat down quietly and had a little rest they might come up to us and say hallo?'

'Of course not, silly boy,' said Deborah. 'Fairies have to be looked for, and I'm going on looking. You can sit down if you like.' And she sat him down by the edge of the grassy path and went on a little way alone.

A moment later she came running back, very excited.

'Guess what, Teddy Robinson!' she called out. 'I've found blackberries, lots and lots of them, and they're all ripe. I'm going to pick a whole bucketful for Auntie Sue.'

'But have you got a whole bucket?' asked Teddy Robinson.

'No, I haven't got anything,' said Deborah, 'and my hands are full already. But I'll run back and get a basket. Will you be a good boy, Teddy Robinson, and sit here till I come back? Promise me not to move.'

'Yes, I promise,' said Teddy Robinson. 'Just put my garland straight before you go, will you?'

So Deborah put his garland straight, then she kissed him good-bye, and ran off down the grassy path.

When she had gone it seemed very quiet in the little green lane. There was no sound at all except the drowsy buzzing of flies, and not a leaf stirred in the green branches overhead. Teddy Robinson sat perfectly still and thought about how quiet it was, and how green it was; and after a while he began to make up a little song about it. It went like this:

'Quiet and green,
quiet and green,
bushes and treeses with grasses between.
Quiet and brown,
quiet and brown,
one teddy bear sitting quietly down;
quiet and brown
in the quiet and green,
all by himself – not a soul to be seen.'

'Except me!' said a tiny voice, and Teddy Robinson saw that a beautiful furry caterpillar was crawling up his leg.

'Hallo!' he said. 'That's a very fine fur coat you are wearing.'

'Yes, isn't it?' said the caterpillar, and he wriggled round so that he could look down his own back and admire it.

'I have a fur coat too,' said Teddy Robinson.

'Have you really?' said the caterpillar. 'Where?'

'You're crawling over it now,' said Teddy Robinson.

'Oh, am I?' said the caterpillar. 'I'm so sorry. I'd no idea. You're so very large I quite thought this was a field I was walking in. I know I came up a very big hill just now.'

'Yes, that was my leg,' said Teddy Robinson.

'Dear me!' said the furry caterpillar. 'Do forgive

me. I wouldn't have walked on your fur coat for anything.' And he hurried away to crawl down the other side.

'Don't mention it,' said Teddy Robinson. 'Please crawl about on me as much as you like. My fur is quite old, and I really don't mind.'

But the caterpillar had gone scrambling down his other leg and was already hurrying away into the grass.

Teddy Robinson began humming to himself again:

'Quiet and green,
 quiet and green,
 bushes and treeses with grasses between . . .'

And then he stopped, because he felt almost sure that while he was humming he had heard other little voices singing different words to the same tune. But as soon as he was quiet everything else was quiet too.

'It must have been a think,' said Teddy Robinson to himself. 'I won't take any notice.'

So he started again:

'Quiet and green,
 quiet and green . . .'

Then he stopped suddenly and listened again. And this time he was quite sure, because the other little voices went on after he had stopped, and this is what they were singing:

'We haven't been seen,
 we haven't been seen;
 creep through the bushes and grasses between.

Better take care!
There's somebody there.
Mind where you step – it's a big brown bear.'

Teddy Robinson held his breath and kept quite still. A moment later he heard a little rustling noise in the grasses behind him, and then a lot of tiny voices all began talking at once.

'It's all right,' said one. 'He isn't fierce.'

'He's wearing flowers round his head,' said another.

'Let's go and have a proper look at him,' said a third.

There was a little more rustling and whispering behind Teddy Robinson, and then out they came. A whole crowd of fairies, not one of them half as big as himself, and all dressed in the prettiest colours he had ever seen, with tiny garlands of flowers round their heads. Teddy Robinson could hardly believe his eyes!

They flitted about in front of him. One or two of them spread their wings and flew a little way here and there. A beautiful little fairy with a star in her hair shook out the frills of her pink and yellow dress. Another, with a garland of forget-me-nots, threw a thistledown in the air and fanned it with her wings. And all the time, out of the corners of their eyes, they were watching Teddy Robinson and whispering about him to each other.

'Look,' said one, who was dressed in a silver cobweb, 'he is wearing a garland like ours. *I* think he might be a fairy person.'

'He couldn't be,' said another. 'His feet are too big.'

'And he isn't wearing a fairy dress,' said a tiny one in rosy pink.

'He is extremely large,' said all the fairies together, and then they all began talking at once again.

'He's bumpy and lumpy.'

'His legs are stumpy.'

'His back's too humpy.'

'His face looks grumpy.'

'It doesn't,' said the cobweb fairy. 'And look, he has lovely soft fur.' And, reaching out a tiny hand, she stroked Teddy Robinson on the tummy. Then another fairy grew brave and came up to touch him, and then another, and another; and soon they were all pulling at his ears and poking him gently with their spiky little fingers.

Teddy Robinson felt a big laugh beginning to rumble inside of him.

'Oh! You're tickling me!' he said.

At once all the fairies flew down, frightened, and stood looking at him from a little way off.

'He has a voice like a thunderstorm,' they said. 'Perhaps he is a new kind of giant.'

Teddy Robinson was pleased at this, but he didn't want to frighten them away, so he said, 'No, I am not a giant.'

'What are you, then?' they asked.

'I'm a bear.'

'A human bear?'

all pulling at his ears and poking him gently

'No, just a teddy bear.'

'Fancy that! Can you fly?'

'No,' said Teddy Robinson. 'I wish I could, but bears don't have wings.'

'Do you wish you were a fairy like us?'

'I don't know,' said Teddy Robinson. 'I quite like being a teddy bear really, but I should *love* to fly. I've always wanted to fly.'

'Come with us to Fairyland, then,' said the fairies. 'Come and live with us, and we will make you a pair of wings.'

'I couldn't come and *live* with you,' said Teddy

Robinson, 'because I live with Deborah. But I should love to come for a visit.'

'Oh, no!' said all the fairies. 'That would never do. If you come with us you must stay for always. Nobody is allowed to come back once they know all the fairy secrets.'

'Then, I'm afraid I can't come,' said Teddy Robinson sadly. 'You see, I couldn't possibly come without Deborah, and she couldn't come, because she has a mummy and daddy who couldn't do without her.'

'But think how lovely it would be,' said the fairy with the star in her hair. 'You would have a beautiful dress like mine, with pink and yellow frills, and you would drink honey out of rose petals, and we should powder your fur with star-dust so that you would shine in the dark. You would have such a lovely time with us you would never miss Deborah at all.'

'Oh, but I should! I know I should!' said Teddy Robinson. 'You see, we are very special to each other. And, anyway, I promised her I would stay sitting here until she came back.

Then all the fairies joined hands in a circle and began to dance round and round Teddy Robinson, singing in tiny little teasing voices:

> 'Teddy bear,
> fat and fair,
> don't be a quite-contrary-bear.
> Fly with us,
> as free as air;
> be a fairy, teddy bear.'

How pretty he too would have looked with a pair of fairy wings

But Teddy Robinson just said, 'No. No. I'm going to stay sitting here like I promised Deborah.'

Then the fairies danced faster and faster round him until their feet weren't even touching the ground; and they all spread out their wings most beautifully until Teddy Robinson thought it was quite the prettiest sight he had ever seen.

He began to have a little think about how pretty he too would have looked with a pair of fairy wings. He began to feel as light as a feather. He forgot about his fat tummy and his big feet, and soon he felt just as if he were floating through the air.

And the fairies, as if they knew all about his little think, began to sing again:

'Airy bear,
fairy bear,
floating lightly in the air,
borne aloft on fairy wings,
while fairies dance in fairy rings,
and every dancing fairy sings,
"Oh, airy, fairy bear!"'

Then, just as Teddy Robinson was thinking he might really take off without meaning to, he heard footsteps coming down the grassy path, and there was Deborah running up to him with the basket in her hand. And in less than a second every single fairy had flown away! Deborah never saw even the end of a fairy's wing. All she saw was her dear old Teddy Robinson sitting just where she had left him by the edge of the grassy path.

'You *are* a good boy,' she said, as she picked him up and hugged him. 'You stayed sitting down just as you promised. I knew you wouldn't run away.'

'So did I,' said Teddy Robinson, 'and I knew I wouldn't walk away, or crawl away, or hop or skip or jump away. But what I *didn't* know was that I should jolly nearly fly away!'

And then while they picked enough blackberries to fill the basket right to the top Teddy Robinson told Deborah all about what had happened to him in the little green lane.

'They were beautiful,' he said. 'They were just like in Auntie Sue's book, and they did have wings, and they did wear garlands, and they did dance all in a ring.'

'I wish I had seen them too,' said Deborah.

'So do I,' said Teddy Robinson. 'But I'll share it with you. You always give me half of anything nice, so I'll give you half of my seeing the fairies, and we'll keep it as a special secret, all to ourselves.'

And that is the end of the story about
Teddy Robinson and the fairies.

8

Teddy Robinson's Dreadful Accident

ONE day Teddy Robinson had a Dreadful Accident, and this is how it happened.

He and Deborah had decided to go for a little walk by themselves; at least, Deborah was going to walk, and Teddy Robinson was going to be pushed in the dolls' pram.

'We will go by the pond,' said Deborah, 'and then you can watch the ducks.'

'That will be nice,' said Teddy Robinson. 'Can I have a pillow behind me?'

'Yes,' said Deborah, 'you shall have the best dolls' pillow with the frill round it.' And she tucked it in behind him, so that he could sit up straight all the way.

The pond where the ducks lived was not very far from home. They had only to go a little way up the road until they came to a steep path, and at the bottom of the path was the duck pond.

Deborah and Teddy Robinson had just reached the top of the steep little path when they met Mary-Anne coming down the road. She too was pushing a dolls' pram, with her beautiful doll, Jacqueline, inside.

Deborah said, 'Hallo, Mary-Anne,' and Mary-

Anne said, 'Hallo, Deborah,' and they both started talking.

Teddy Robinson looked at Jacqueline, but he didn't say hallo to her, because she was lying down with her eyes shut and he thought she might be asleep. She was covered with a pink satin eiderdown which matched her pink silk dress.

Deborah and Mary-Anne talked to each other until Teddy Robinson was nearly growing tired of waiting; and then, just as they were saying good-bye at last, the Dreadful Accident happened.

A little wind blew up and lifted the eiderdown right off Jacqueline, and sent it spinning away down the road. Deborah said, 'Oh, look! Your eiderdown!' and ran to catch it. And Teddy Robinson found that now Deborah had let go of the pram it was beginning to run downhill all by itself with him inside it.

Bumpety-bump it went, down the steep little path, faster and faster.

'Oh, my goodness!' said Teddy Robinson to himself. 'I hope we shan't bump into that lamp-post at the bottom.'

But that is just what they did. They went *crash* into the lamp-post, the pram turned sideways, and before you could say 'Teddy Robinson' it had shot under the railings and gone *splash* into the pond.

Luckily for Teddy Robinson he fell out as the pram turned over, and a moment later he found himself lying in the mud at the edge of the pond. But the pram was upside down in the water with its wheels

— down the steep little path, faster and faster —

sticking up in the air, and the pillow was floating away.

'Goodness me!' said he. 'What a lucky thing I fell out!'

In another moment he heard Deborah come rushing down the steep little hill, shouting, 'Teddy Robinson! Where are you? Oh, where are you?' And then he saw her frightened face looking at him through the railings over his head.

'Oh, what are we to do?' she cried. 'How ever shall I get you out? Are you drowned? Oh, what a dreadful accident!'

'No, I aren't drowned,' said Teddy Robinson. 'Don't cry. I'm quite all right really, but just run home and ask Mummy to come and get me out.'

So Deborah ran off home as fast as she could, and Teddy Robinson lay in the mud and waited to be rescued.

Before long a duck came swimming over from the other side of the pond. As soon as it saw Teddy Robinson in the mud, and the pram upside down in the water, it said, 'Quack!' in a very loud and surprised voice. Then it turned round and swam quickly back to tell the other ducks.

Teddy Robinson could hear them all quacking together over on the other side of the pond.

'Quack! Quack! He's flat on his back!'

'Who is? And where?'

'The bear, over there.'

'Alas and alack! Who'll fetch him back?'

They crowded round him.

'Quick! Quick! Quack-quack-quack!'

And then they all came swimming over together and crowded round him, asking him questions, and making a great deal of noise to show how worried they were.

Teddy Robinson told them what had happened.

'How awful!' they quacked. 'What a dreadful thing! Fancy that! You'll never be the same again! Poor thing! Oh, quack-quack-quack!'

'I do feel rather wet and muddy,' said Teddy Robinson, 'but I don't think I'm as bad as all that.'

'But you've grown so *thin*!' quacked one duck.

'And such a queer *colour*!' quacked another.

'And your *eyes* are so starey!' quacked a third.

'Have I really? Are they truly?' said Teddy Robinson, and he began to feel rather worried.

'If I could only sit up perhaps I could see my

reflection in the water,' he said, 'and then I should know how bad I am.'

So the kind ducks pushed him gently with their bills until he was sitting upright, and Teddy Robinson looked down into the water. He couldn't see himself very clearly, because a little breeze was rippling over the top of the pond, but he was glad to see that he was all in one piece.

'I do look rather *trembly*,' he said, 'but I think it was only the shock. I had rather a fright, you know.'

'Yes! Yes! A terrible fright!' quacked the ducks. 'What a shock! What a shock! Quack! Quack!'

"I do look rather trembly."

'But I think I'm all right now,' said Teddy Robinson, 'and somebody's coming to fetch me soon.'

'Then, *we* must look after you until they come!' quacked the ducks, and they all crowded round him, quacking and fussing, and trying to be helpful.

'Now, what would you like to eat?' they asked. 'What about a little water weed? Not too much, but a nice little slimy piece?'

'Oh, no, thank you, I really couldn't,' said Teddy Robinson.

'Well, then, you must have plenty of fresh air!' they quacked, and they all began flapping their wings up and down and fanning him.

'It's very kind of you,' said Teddy Robinson, 'but really I'm cold enough already.'

'Then, we must keep you warm!' quacked the ducks, and they all sat on top of him, spreading out their feathers.

'I don't like to mention it,' said Teddy Robinson, 'but your feet are awfully muddy, and I'm so muddy already it seems a pity to make it worse.'

'Yes! Yes! So you are!' quacked the ducks. 'Perhaps we had better wash you!' And they all began pushing him towards the water with their bills.

But at that minute Teddy Robinson heard the sound of voices coming down the path, so he was glad to be able to say, 'Please don't bother! I can hear my people coming to fetch me. Thank you all very much indeed, but I shall be all right now. And, by the way, if any of you would like a little pillow you'll find one floating over there by the reeds.'

'Oh, thank you!' quacked the ducks. 'Just what we should like for our nests. Thank you! Good-bye! Quack! Quack!'

Then along came Deborah and Mummy, and Teddy Robinson was lifted up and passed through the railings, and the pram was lifted out of the water and turned the right way up.

Deborah carried Teddy Robinson home, holding him carefully, because he was so wet and muddy, and looking at him with a worried face, because somehow he looked so different. Mummy wheeled the pram along behind.

'My poor boy!' said Deborah. 'You look terribly thin, and your beautiful fur has all gone, and why are your eyes so round and surprised?'

'Because I had such a dreadful fright,' said Teddy Robinson.

'No, it's only because he is wet,' said Mummy. 'We will wash him when we get home. And don't worry about his fur. I'm sure it will come up nice and fluffy when it's dry again, and then he will look like his old self.'

'But I *did* have a fright,' said Teddy Robinson. 'She might be quite right, but I *did* have a fright.'

'Yes, I'm sure you did,' said Deborah.

So when they got home Teddy Robinson was given a bath in warm soapy water. Then Mummy spread a cloth on top of the cooker, where the plates were usually put to keep warm, and he sat up there to dry.

'Are you comfy?' asked Deborah.

'I *did* have a fright,' he kept saying. 'I *did* have a fright. What a crash! What a smash! What a splish-splosh-splash!'

'Now, for goodness' sake stop talking about it,' said Deborah. 'It's all over now, so you must forget about it.'

'But I don't want to forget about it yet,' said Teddy Robinson. 'It gives me a fright every time I think about it, so I want to go on talking about it until it stops frightening me; otherwise I might think about it by mistake some time, and it would give me a fright when I wasn't looking.'

So he sat on top of the cooker and remembered it out loud four times over from beginning to end. Then he felt better.

'I think I'll come down now,' he said.

'Are you dry?'

'Not quite, but I think it would be nice to sit in front of the fire with the dolls and tell them all about it. I feel as if I could enjoy it now. You haven't told them already, have you?'

'No,' said Deborah. 'I'll get them out of the toy-cupboard.'

So out they all came, and they sat on the hearth-rug in a circle, and Teddy Robinson sat in the middle of them with his back to the fire, and felt very cosy and important.

"Why is your fur so spiky?"

'Oh, Teddy Robinson!' said all the dolls. 'What has been happening to you? Why is your fur so spiky? Have you been swimming? Why are you sitting on a bath-towel?'

'I have been in a Dreadful Accident,' said Teddy Robinson, 'and I thought you might like to hear about it.'

'Oh, yes! Tell us all about it, Teddy Robinson,' said the dolls.

So Teddy Robinson said in a deep and important voice:

> 'Behold the bear
> who had a big scare,
> who rolled in the pram
> from here to there –'

'What! *Our* pram?' asked the dolls.

'Yes,' said Teddy Robinson. 'Don't interrupt.

> 'Behold the bear
> who went with a thud
> over the bank
> and into the mud –'

'What mud? Where?' asked the dolls.

'*Don't interrupt*,' said Teddy Robinson, 'and I'll tell you.

> 'Rolled in the pram
> with a smash and a crash
> into the pond
> with a splish-splosh-splash –'

'Good gracious!' cried all the dolls. 'Tell us about it from the beginning.'

So Teddy Robinson told them the whole story, and the dolls listened right to the end without interrupting once more.

When he had finished they all said, 'How brave you are, Teddy Robinson!'

'But didn't you *do* anything?' asked one of them. 'Do you mean you just lay there and waited?'

'Sometimes that is the bravest thing you *can* do,' said Teddy Robinson, 'just stay where you are and wait to be found.'

'Yes,' said all the other dolls, 'Teddy Robinson is quite right. How very brave he is!'

'And now,' said Teddy Robinson, 'I think it's time I was turned round. I seem to be nicely browned on that side.'

"My fur has never looked so nice before"

So Deborah turned him round until his other side was quite dry too, then she brushed his fur with the dolls' hairbrush. It came up so beautifully soft and fluffy that it looked just like new. Deborah was quite excited.

'You *do* look lovely!' she cried. 'Mummy said you would look like your old self again when your fur was dry; but it's even better than that – you look like your *new* self!'

And she held him up in front of the mirror so that he could see himself.

'Oh, I do, don't I?' said Teddy Robinson. 'I *am* glad I had that Dreadful Accident. It has made me feel quite special and important, and my fur has never looked so nice before.'

'Not since it was new,' said Deborah.

'No,' he said, 'and we wouldn't have noticed it so much then, because we didn't know each other so well, did we?'

And that is the end of the story about Teddy Robinson's dreadful accident.

9

Teddy Robinson Has a Holiday

ONE day in summer it was very, very hot. Teddy
Robinson sat on the window-sill in Deborah's room
and said to himself, 'Phew! Phew! I wish I could
take my fur coat off. It *is* a hot day!'

Deborah came running in from the garden to fetch
her sun hat. When she saw Teddy Robinson sitting
all humpy and hot on the window-sill she said,
'Never mind, poor boy. You'll be cooler when you
have your holiday.'

'Are I going to have a holiday?' said Teddy
Robinson.

'Yes, of course you are,' said Deborah.

'When will it come?' said Teddy Robinson.

'Very soon now,' said Deborah, and she ran out
into the garden again.

Teddy Robinson sat and thought about this for a
long while. He knew he had heard the word 'holiday'
before, but he just could not remember what it
meant.

'Now, I wonder what a holiday can be,' he said to
himself. 'She said I would be cooler when I had it. Is
it a teddy bear's sun-suit perhaps? Or a little um-
brella? Or could it be a long, cold drink in a glass
with a straw? And she said it would come very soon.

But how will it come? Will it come in a box tied up with ribbon? Or on a tray? Or will the postman bring it in a parcel? Or will it just come walking in all by itself?'

Teddy Robinson didn't know the answer to any of these questions, so be began singing a little song to himself.

'I'm going to have a holiday,
a holiday,
a holiday.
I'm going to have a holiday.
How lucky I shall be.

What ever *is* a holiday,
a holiday,
a holiday?
What ever *is* a holiday?
I'll have to wait and see.'

'Yes,' he said to himself, 'I'll have to wait and see. I'll ask Deborah about it tomorrow.'

But when tomorrow came all sorts of exciting things began to happen, so Teddy Robinson forgot to ask Deborah after all.

Daddy brought a big trunk down from the attic, and Mummy began packing it with clothes and shoes, and Deborah turned everything out of her toy cupboard on to the floor, and began looking for her bucket and spade.

'What is going to happen?' asked Teddy Robinson. 'Are we going away?'

'Yes, of course we are,' said Deborah. 'We're going to the seaside. I told you yesterday.'

'How funny. I didn't know,' said Teddy Robinson.

'That's why everything is going in the trunk,' said Deborah. 'To go to the seaside!'

'Us too?' said Teddy Robinson.

'No,' said Deborah. 'We shall go in a train. Now, be a good boy and help me tidy up all these toys. I've found my bucket and spade.'

So together they tidied up the toys. Then they said good-bye to all the dolls and put them to bed in the toy cupboard.

At last there was nothing left on the floor at all, except one tiny little round glass thing that Teddy Robinson found lying close beside him. It was about as big as a sixpence, and was a beautiful golden brown colour, with a black blob in the middle.

He showed it to Deborah.

'Now, I wonder what ever that can be,' she said. 'It can't be a bead, because it hasn't got a hole through the middle.'

'And it can't be a marble,' said Teddy Robinson, 'because it's flat on one side.'

'Perhaps it's a sweet,' said Deborah.

'Suck it and see,' said Teddy Robinson.

'I mustn't suck it in case it's poison,' said Deborah. So she licked it instead.

'No,' she said, 'it isn't a sweet, because it hasn't got any taste.'

"Now I wonder what ever that can be"

'It's very pretty,' said Teddy Robinson. 'Shall we keep it?'

'Yes,' said Deborah. 'It's too pretty to throw away. I wish I could think what it is, though. I'm sure I've seen it before somewhere, but I can't remember where.'

'That's funny,' said Teddy Robinson. 'I was thinking just the same thing.'

Before they went to bed that night they dropped the pretty little round thing (that wasn't a marble, and wasn't a bead, and wasn't a sweet) through the slot in Deborah's money-box.

'That will be a safe place to keep it,' said Deborah.

And the very next day they all went away to the seaside.

Teddy Robinson enjoyed the ride in the train very much, because he was allowed to sit in the rack and look after the luggage. And Deborah enjoyed it very much, because they had a picnic dinner in the train, and it was so lovely to be able to look out of the window and watch the cows in the fields and eat a hard-boiled egg in her fingers at the same time.

It wasn't until they were quite half-way there that things began to go wrong.

Daddy lifted Teddy Robinson down from the rack. He was just going to give him to Deborah when he looked at him closely and said, 'Hallo, old man, what's happened to your other eye?'

'Oh dear,' said Mummy. 'Is it loose? I shall have to sew it on again before it gets lost.'

'No, it isn't here,' said Daddy.

'Oh dear! Oh dear!' said Deborah. 'Let me see. Oh, you poor boy! What are we to do? Wherever can it be?'

They all began looking round the railway carriage and in the corners of the seats, but the other eye was nowhere to be seen.

Deborah lifted Teddy Robinson on to her lap to comfort him and looked sadly into his one eye. Suddenly she said, 'Teddy Robinson! Do you remember the pretty little round glass thing we found yesterday?'

'The thing that wasn't a bead, and wasn't a marble, and wasn't a sweet?' said Teddy Robinson.

'Yes,' said Deborah. 'Well, that was your eye! This one is just the same. Fancy my not knowing it when I saw it!'

'And it's in the money-box,' said Teddy Robinson sadly.

'Oh dear, so it is!' said Deborah. 'Whatever shall we do?'

'Stop the train!' said Teddy Robinson. 'We must go home and fetch it at once.'

But they couldn't stop the train. Daddy and Mummy both said they couldn't. So Teddy Robinson sat in the corner seat and grumbled to himself quietly while Deborah tried to comfort him by telling him about the nice time he was going to have at the seaside.

'We'll go down to the beach every day,' she said, 'and you shall come with me. Don't mind about your

"Stop the train!"

cye too much. You shall have it as soon as we get home.'

'But I can't go down to the beach with only one eye,' said Teddy Robinson.

'Yes, you can,' said Deborah. 'No one will notice.'

'No, I can't,' said Teddy Robinson. 'There will be other children on the beach. If I can't go with two eyes I won't go at all.'

'Oh, Teddy Robinson,' said Deborah. 'What am I to do with you?'

'I know!' said Daddy. 'Make him into a pirate. Pirates always wear a patch over one eye. Then no one will know.'

'Yes,' said Mummy. 'What a good idea! And he can wear my red-and-white spotted handkerchief round his head.'

'And he can wear curtain rings for ear-rings,' said Deborah. 'Yes, that *is* a good idea.'

Teddy Robinson began to feel much happier, and by the time the train came into the station his one eye was twinkling as usual, and he felt as pleased as Deborah to think they were really at the seaside at last.

As soon as breakfast was over the next morning Teddy Robinson and Deborah got ready to go down to the beach.

Deborah wore shorts and a T-shirt, and Teddy Robinson wore his trousers and no shirt. Mummy fixed the patch over his eye, and hung two gold curtain rings over his ears with pieces of cotton. Then she tied her red-and-white spotted handkerchief round his head.

'There, now,' she said; 'doesn't he look exactly like a pirate?' And she called Daddy to come and see.

'My word!' said Daddy. 'I hope he won't frighten everybody away!'

On the way down to the beach Teddy Robinson said to Deborah, 'Do I really look like a pirate?'

'Yes,' said Deborah, 'you really do.'

'What *is* a pirate?' asked Teddy Robinson.

'He's a fierce robber man who lives in a ship,' said Deborah.

'Oh, goody! I love being fierce,' said Teddy Robinson. 'And who do I rob?'

'Other people who live in other ships,' said Deborah.

'That will be very nice,' said Teddy Robinson. 'I hope there will be plenty of other people in other ships there.'

But when they got down to the beach they found that the other people were mostly sitting about in deckchairs or walking about on the sands.

'I can't very well rob people who're sitting in deckchairs, can I?' said Teddy Robinson. 'And I don't think I should look quite right sitting in one myself.'

So Daddy and Deborah made a big sand-castle down by the edge of the sea, and when it was finished they sat Teddy Robinson on top of it.

'There,' said Deborah. 'Your ship has been

wrecked and sunk to the bottom of the sea, but you are safe on a desert island all of your own. Now you don't mind if I go and play with the other children, do you?'

Teddy Robinson didn't mind a bit. When Deborah had gone he sat on top of his sand-castle island and looked out to sea, feeling very fierce and brave.

He watched the seagulls flying and diving over the waves. After a while one of them came flying round and swooped down quite close to his head, screaming at him. It sounded very fierce, but Teddy Robinson didn't mind because he was feeling fierce too.

'Who are you-ou-ou?' screamed the seagull. 'And what are you doing here?'

'I'm a pirate,' shouted Teddy Robinson, 'and I'm

"I'm not afraid of you even if you do scream at me"

It looked up at him with cross black eyes

not afraid of you, even if you do scream at me. This
is my very own island, and you can't come on it.'

The seagull screamed at him again and flew away.

Then a crab came waddling round the sand-castle
island. It walked sideways and looked up at Teddy
Robinson with cross black eyes.

'Who are you?' said the crab. 'And what are you
doing on my beach?'

'I'm a pirate,' roared Teddy Robinson in a big,
brave bear's voice, 'and I'm not afraid of you, even
if you do walk sideways and stare at me with a cross
face. And this is *my* island, so you can't come on it
unless I invite you.'

'Are you going to invite me?' said the crab.

'Not unless you stop looking so cross,' said Teddy
Robinson.

'Then I shan't come,' said the crab. 'If I want to be cross I *shall* be cross, and even a pirate can't stop me.'

And he scuttled away into the sand.

Teddy Robinson felt very happy indeed. There was nothing he liked better than spending a beautiful, fierce morning all by himself at the seaside.

He began singing about it as loudly as he could.

> 'Look at me
> beside the sea,
> the one-eyed pirate bear!
> You'll never be
> as fierce as me,
> so fight me if you dare!'

Just then a big black dog came running down the beach and began barking loudly at Teddy Robinson.

'Woof! Woof! What are you doing?' he barked.

'I'm a pirate on a desert island,' shouted Teddy Robinson, 'and you can't frighten me, even if you do bark at me so rudely.'

'Woof! Woof!' barked the dog. 'You certainly are on an island. Look, there's water all round you.'

'Good gracious, so there is!' said Teddy Robinson. 'However did that happen?'

'I expect the tide came up when you weren't looking,' said the big black dog. 'Woof! Woof! Shall I save you?'

'No, thank you,' said Teddy Robinson. 'Pirates don't need to be saved. But thank you for telling me.'

"You certainly are on an island!"

He was just beginning to wonder how he was going to get back to the beach all by himself when Deborah came running up and paddled out to the castle to fetch him.

'Oh, Teddy Robinson!' she said. 'I heard the dog barking, and I got quite a fright when I saw you sitting with the water all round you. Were you frightened when you saw the tide was coming up?'

'Of course I weren't,' said Teddy Robinson. 'Pirates aren't frightened. I was just looking out to sea with my one brave eye and I never even noticed it. You know, I'm very fond of my other eye, but I'm rather glad we left it at home after all. I do so like being a pirate at the seaside. Can I have a castle to myself every day?'

'Yes, every day till we go home,' said Deborah. 'But next time we won't put it quite so near the edge of the water.'

When at last the holiday was over and they all went home again Teddy Robinson was quite excited to find his other eye still inside Deborah's money-box, and to have it sewn on again. He and Deborah both felt as if they had been away for years and years, because every one at home seemed so pleased to see them again.

'How big you've grown!' they all said to Deborah, and 'How brown you are!' they all said to Teddy Robinson. 'What a lovely holiday you must have had.'

'Oh! My holiday!' said Teddy Robinson. 'I'd forgotten all about it!'

'What do you mean?' said Deborah.

'Well, I never had it, did I?' said Teddy Robinson. 'Did it come while we were at the seaside?'

'Of course it did,' said Deborah. 'That *was* your holiday – going to the seaside.'

'Well, I never!' said Teddy Robinson. 'Was it really? Oh, I *am* glad if *that* was my holiday. I never thought it would be anything as nice as that!'

And that is the end of the story about how
Teddy Robinson had a holiday.

About the Author

Joan G. Robinson was born at Gerrards Cross, and attended seven schools in all. She became an illustrator, and then took to writing – when the business of home-running allowed. Apart from the Teddy Robinson books, she also wrote *When Marnie was There*, *Charley*, *The House in the Square* and the *Mary Mary* books, and they have all been translated into several languages and been dramatized on radio and television.

She is married and has two daughters, and now lives in London and in Norfolk. Of Teddy Robinson she says: 'His adventures might happen to anyone's teddy bear, but his way of looking at them is his own.'

THE ADVENTURES OF UNCLE LUBIN
W. Heath Robinson

The amazing adventures of good old Uncle Lubin in his search for his little nephew, Peter, who has been stolen by the wicked Bag-bird. With the author's own unforgettable illustrations.

DAVID AND HIS GRANDFATHER
Pamela Rogers

Three long stories about David and his kind, friendly Grandfather, who participates in all his secret schemes.

JACKO AND OTHER STORIES
Jean Sutcliffe

Stories about pets and people by an expert who is really in touch with young children – the creator of the *Listen With Mother* programme.

THE OWL WHO WAS AFRAID
OF THE DARK
Jill Tomlinson

Being afraid of the dark has its problems, especially when you're a baby owl, but Plop comes to learn that the dark can be exciting, fun, beautiful and a lot else besides.

THE PENNY PONY
Barbara Willard

Life is never quite the same for Cathy and Roger after they find the penny pony in Mrs Boddy's shop.

FANTASTIC MR FOX
Roald Dahl

Every evening Mr Fox would creep down into the valley in the darkness and help himself to a nice plump chicken, duck or turkey, but there came a day when Farmers Boggis, Bunce and Bean determined to stop him whatever the cost ...

PLAYTIME STORIES
Joyce Donoghue

Everyday children in everyday situations – these are stories for parents to read aloud and share with their children.

TALES OF JOE AND TIMOTHY
JOE AND TIMOTHY TOGETHER
Dorothy Edwards

Friendly, interesting stories about two small boys living in different flats in a tall, tall house, and the good times they have together. By the author of the *Naughty Little Sister* stories.

THE ANITA HEWETT ANIMAL STORY BOOK

A collection of cheerful, funny, varied animal stories from all over the world. Ideal for reading aloud to children of 5 or 6.

THE SHRINKING OF TREEHORN
Florence Parry Heide

'Nobody shrinks!' declared Treehorn's father, but Treehorn *was* shrinking, and it wasn't long before even the unshakeable adults had to admit it.

EMILY'S VOYAGE
Emma Smith

Emily Guinea-Pig leaves her cosy home to go on her first sea voyage – only to be shipwrecked on a tropical island with the crew of frightened rabbits and their lackadaisical captain.

CLEVER POLLY AND THE STUPID WOLF
POLLY AND THE WOLF AGAIN
Catherine Storr

Clever Polly manages to think of lots of good ideas to stop the stupid wolf from eating her.

BAD BOYS
ed. Eileen Colwell

Twelve splendid stories about naughty boys, by favourite authors like Helen Cresswell, Charlotte Hough, Barbara Softly and Ursula Moray Williams.

DUGGIE THE DIGGER AND HIS FRIENDS
Michael Prescott

As well as Duggie the Digger, there are tales about Horace the Helicopter, Bertram the Bus and Vernon the Vacuum Cleaner. It will please little boys who are interested in mechanical things.

If you have enjoyed this book and would like to know about others which we publish, why not join the Puffin Club? You will receive the club magazine, *Puffin Post*, four times a year and a smart badge and membership book. You will also be able to enter all competitions. For details of cost and an application form send a stamped addressed envelope to:

The Puffin Club, Dept. A
Penguin Books Limited
Bath Road
Harmondsworth
Middlesex